FORBIDDEN
Part 1
By Edmond White

Dedication

First and foremost, I would like to thank God for giving me the knowledge and insight to create another story. My first novel, "A Second Chance, is doing fairly well. I would like to thank each of you who has purchased my first book. It means the world to me. I have received positive responses from friends, family, and readers from all over the world. I write stories to detach you from busy lifestyles without leaving your surroundings. A glimpse into another person's struggles can often help us with what we have in front of us and be thankful for it. "Forbidden" is part one of three installments. I hope you enjoy it. And once again, thanks so much for your support!

Table of contents:

PROLOGUE

For the lips of a strange woman drop as honeycomb, and her mouth is smoother than oil:
But her end is bitter as wormwood, sharp as a two-edged sword. Her feet go down to death; her steps
Take hold of Hell.
Proverbs 5:3

CHAPTER 1

My name is Julius Anderson. Everyone calls me J. My wedding is one month from today. When my friends and family discovered the news, they were highly overjoyed and a tad bit skeptical at the same time. I've never been one to settle down. The idea of being with one woman for the rest of my life petrifies me. I cannot grasp how two people can live together for the rest of their lives without growing weary of one another. The ball and chain routine is not my thing. My family knows I'm certainly not that person. I change women like I change my socks. I've been with amazing women willing to do anything for me if I asked them to. When I met Maya at twenty-seven, I was tired of bouncing around from bed to bed. I assumed it would never happen to me, but I needed to feel a connection with someone. My brain needed stimulation just as much as other areas. When Maya walked into my life, I felt this fantastic assemblage. She has everything I desire in a woman.

She is sexy, intelligent, outgoing, and has a stimulating conversation. Sometimes, I believe she's my twin. We even think on the same level. She's a beautiful person inside and out. I don't have any second thoughts of being with her. I honestly believe she is the one for me, but on the other hand, I have a severe problem jeopardizing my marriage to Maya. I guess you can say my interest in the opposite sex started early. Forrt, my mother paI remember reading me around tow,n showing me off to her family and friends. She was so proud of my appearance and never missed an opportunity to let others know how she felt about me. She clothed me in the most expensive threads and would spend half her paycheck on an outfit for me that would set her back on her bills for at least a couple of weeks. In her opinion, looks mean everything. My mother would tell me that if you look good, people will think your life is in perfect order.

A far cry from what it is at this moment? Beauty is in the eye of the beholder to some extent when it comes to adoration from others. How does anyone know their actual appearance if not by feedback from others? Responses from others can be an influential tool for a man or a woman to live by. In my case, the positive responses are constant. Since age five, I have always experienced kind gestures from the opposite sex. Women usually immediately notice me, whether it's a wink, smile, or a warm statement. People tell me I resemble the England-born Idris Elba to some extent. I've heard it so much that on some occasions, I try to emulate his accent when amongst friends just to make them laugh. I think I look like a combination of my mother and father. My mother has smooth cocoa butter skin and crafty, enticing dark brown eyes. My dad's skin is rich dark chocolate, and his eyes are a masculine light brown.

Back in my teens, I dated so many girls that I lost count. I'm very fortunate not to have any starving children running around. I heeded my father's "protect yourself before you wreck yourself" motto. I've never entered a girl without wearing a condom, a rule I currently live by. It bothers my fiance, the fact that I continue to use condoms in our two-year relationship. It angers her every time I put one on. Often, it takes her out of the mood, and then we start yelling at each other. It was never a problem at the beginning of our relationship, but as of late, it has become a significant issue.

I think she wants me to give her a child. Her hints have become more determined as of late. Her Children's Place Magazine subscription has been coming monthly in the mail like clockwork. The magazines sit in a semicircle on top of the living room table. She volunteers to watch her sister's son whenever we go out. If I refuse to help her, it becomes another form of an argument in which I give in just to make things go smoothly between us. Her nephew is only eight months old. When it's time to change his diaper, she says I should watch her and learn for the future. Getting her pregnant is the least of my problems at this point. If I could do it all over again, I can't. My indiscretion is destroying me. Whenever I look at Maya, I want to tell her what's happening. I want to be upfront with her and put all my cards on the table. I'm just too afraid to hurt her. I've never meant to do her like this.

Jodie Stevens is Maya's girlfriend. They have been friends since college. A day doesn't pass without Maya speaking to Jodie over the phone. Jodie lives fifteen minutes away from us. She comes over early every morning so she and Maya can get their daily jog before heading to work. In college, they both ran track together. Maya was the short-distance sprinter, whereas Jodie ran the longer distance for cross country. Their lean bodies haven't changed much since college. Maya has a petite shape with noticeable curves and lean-toned legs. I will never grow weary of her golden-brown complexion and hazel eyes. She's simply beautiful.

I enjoy her company, and she certainly makes me happy. Now, describing her friend Jodie is like comparing last year's model car to this year's newer model. Whatever Maya has in looks, Jodie's version is ten times better. Her tight figure, perfect dimples, and striking facial features are stunning. When Maya first introduced me to her, I stared at her uncontrollably. I didn't want to be evident with Maya sitting beside me, but it was challenging to stop staring at her. When she shook my hand, it was hard for me to let go of hers. Her penetrating green eyes had me open. It was almost mind-altering how she made me feel. As stated earlier, my Idris Elba appeal usually makes most women croon over me. I never have to do much to get a woman's attention except smile. Customarily, I am never the hunter, but Jodie is appealing. From then on, I would be in the same room whenever I knew Jodie was coming by the apartment. I realize I have it bad for her. The more I try to ignore her, the more she remains in my thoughts. I assume her feelings are on the same level as mine. When visiting Maya, she makes subtle advances I cannot overlook.

Our affair happened one morning when Jodie came by the apartment to go running with Maya. Jodie usually visits without ever calling first. She didn't know Maya was under the weather with a temperature 102. It seemed Maya had forgotten to call her, being sick and all. Maya drank plenty of fluids, and I checked on her periodically that morning. When the doorbell sounded, my heart went into overdrive. My throat became parched, and I wanted nothing but her body. I anticipated what would happen when I opened the door. I peeked through the peephole, becoming aroused by the sight of her as she stood there in front of our doorway wearing black running tights and a gray sports bra, her long blonde mane tied into a ponytail. My earlier escapades with females never involved a Caucasian woman. I didn't know what to expect.

Nonetheless, my lust for her overrode my slight uncertainty. Jodie isn't your typical white female, and she's been around African Americans her entire life. Jodie has attended all-black schools and dates nothing but brotha's. She was adopted as a baby by a loving African-American family. Jodie is one of three children they have adopted.

I could feel our energy for each other when I opened the door. Jodie stood in the doorway, staring back at me. I didn't waste any time. I grabbed her by the waist, pulling her in closer to me. Her tantalizing perfume stung my nostrils. I guided her inside the doorway, silently closing the door while keeping my face buried in her aroma. I kissed and squeezed her like our world was coming to an end. She moaned for me. Jodie removed the rubber band, holding her ponytail and letting her hair fall past her shoulders. I rubbed my hands through her hair, biting her neck gently. Her moans intensified. I gently covered her mouth with my hand so Maya wouldn't hear. She then seductively kissed my fingers, and the softness of her lips sent my hormones into overdrive. What we did next was take a huge risk. Our lust for each other ignored every red flag imaginable. We stripped off our clothing and made love inside Maya's apartment. This affair of ours has been going on for the past six months. Jodie has complete control over me. I don't know how it happened, but it has. I think about her more than I think about Maya. Just last weekend, Jodie called Maya and told her she had something important to share.

Before that call, Jodie had kept her distance from me for several weeks. She doesn't come by the house as often as before our affair. I asked Maya one evening why Jodie hadn't been showing up to run in the mornings. Maya said Jodie has a calf sprain and is nursing her injury. Jodie declined to share her number with me. She said it was too risky, plus Maya might find out by checking my outgoing calls. I somewhat agreed.

Nevertheless, I needed to speak with her. I had to find out what was going on. So I took it upon myself to scroll through Maya's cell to find Jodie's number. Once I found the number, I called her immediately, blocking my number. With every ring, my heart rate wavered. I was nervous and excited at the same time. I wanted to hear her voice and feel reassured she hadn't forgotten about me. So you can imagine my dismay when a man's voice came through the phone instead of Jodie's. He said hello three times before I ended the call. I stood there staring at my cell phone in open suspicion. Jodie never told me she had a boyfriend. I assumed she was single. At least, that's what Maya told me. As I sit in the living room, I wonder what's so important that Jodie has to come over and tell Maya. Why couldn't she tell her over the phone? Is she planning to inform Maya about our affair? Something just doesn't feel right to me. The last time we made love to each other, she seemed detached. I hope she isn't having second thoughts. Maya is in the kitchen finishing up dinner before Jodie arrives. I'm panicky, and my stomach is in knots. I don't know how to react when she comes through the door. I begin to sweat. I turn on the AC, allowing the room to cool off as well as myself. Maya walks inside the living room.

"The air feels good in here. I don't know how long this heatwave is going to last. Honey, are you alright?" She asks with a confounded expression.

"I'm fine, Maya. Why do you ask?"

"It looks like something is bothering you," she plops down on my lap. I look into her hazel eyes, giving her a soft kiss on her lips.

"I'm cool, Maya. It's just humid in here. The humidity has me kind of drained out."

"So, what do you think it is?" She softly caresses my face.

"What are you talking about?" She gives me a quizzical look.

"The thing Jodie has to tell me, silly?" I quickly move her off my lap and head for the AC unit.

"I don't know. Why are you asking me?" She twists her head to the side, frowning at me.

"What's with you?"

"Nothing, I'm good."

"Then why did you jump up off the couch like that? Did my question offend you in some kind of way?" *I didn't realize what I just did. Jodie has me so caught up. I'm on the edge because of her. My reaction certainly wasn't brilliant in front of Maya.*

"I... just needed some air. The AC isn't blowing out cool air like it should be. I think we need a new one," I place my hand in front of the vent.

"It feels fine to me, Julius," her unsettling stare makes me anxious.

"Are you sure?"

"Yes, don't waste more money on a new unit. This one works just fine," I sit back on the sofa.

"You never know with Jodie, Maya. It can be anything. She's always surprising you with something."

"I know. Jodie's always doing nice things for me. I hope she didn't buy anything for this apartment. She's constantly decorating."

"She's an interior designer. It's what she does."

"Well, she needs to stop. We already have more than enough in here. Don't you think so, Julius?"

"Yeah, we don't have room for anything else in this place."

"You know something? She's been acting a little bizarre lately."

"What makes you believe that?"

"I've known her since college. I think she has someone in her life. When she meets someone, she usually keeps her distance. Jodie pours herself into her significant other. If she likes you, she caters to your every need. I always tell her to be careful because she gets bored easily. I don't want her hurting or hurting someone else."

"Why does she get bored so easily?" I ask uncomfortably.

"Just look at her, Julius. Jodie is a bombshell of a woman. I wish I had the development she has. She usually has men eating out the palm of her hand in no time. They want to marry her, take her away, and buy her everything. All of that doesn't matter to her, though. She likes challenges. I've seen men rejected by her afterward crying like children, all because she didn't want them anymore. Men get hysterical over Jodie. I gave her the thenicknameePoisonn, like the Bell, Biv, and Devoe song. You can't trust a big but and a smile," she laughs. *Maya's words are disturbing to me. I have some symptoms she just described about Jodie's past boyfriends. Has she dumped me already? It's only been six months, and I must admit the best six months of my life. I don't know what to do if I can't see her anymore. It's probably something else she has to share with Maya. I hope. She's never mentioned anyone else to me. Then again, I never asked her either. I hope Maya is wrong. The thought of Jodie being with someone else is too complex to swallow. Making love is like a volcanic eruption when we're together. I swear I can't get enough of her.*

"This guy you're assuming she's with, do you honestly think she'll stay with him?"

"If she does, it will be news to me. I mean, it's not in her character. She likes the excitement in the beginning when things are fresh. Jodie dislikes the work required to maintain a relationship. It's always been that way with her. I don't think she'll ever change."

"What's the longest relationship she's been in?" Maya sits back on my lap.

"I would say a year," she frowns.

"Why, the twenty questions?" Maya scans my face for an answer.

"I only asked a few questions. I know Jodie's your girl and everything. I was just making conversation."

"Um, hmm, I see how you look at her, J. You want her, don't you?" She gets off my lap and stands up, glaring at me with her hands on her hips.

"How can you ask me that? We're getting married in a month. Did you forget already?"

"That doesn't mean shit to me, J. As long as you men can get a piece, the occasion doesn't matter. Whenever she's here, I see how you look at her, J. I know she's beautiful, but you can at least respect me. I'm your fiancé Julius!" She screams. *I feel ashamed of how I disrespected Maya. Sleeping with your woman's friend is one of the lowest things a man can do. There's no sound explanation or legitimate reason to explain it. I've been disloyal to her, and the sad thing is I can't stop doing it. I love Maya entirely and want us to grow as a couple. It Sounds unreasonable to say I love her while sleeping with her friend, but I do love her. I just can't seem to turn off my feelings for Jodie.*

"Baby, listen to me; if I stared at her in your presence, I'm sorry. It won't happen again. I probably did it without realizing it."

"Save that shit for someone else, J. Is that supposed to make me feel better because you didn't realize it?" I get off the sofa, reaching out for her hand. She moves away from me.

"I won't stare at her anymore. I'm sorry if I offended you," she rolls her eyes.

"You had better get it right, or you will be standing at the altar by yourself. I will not be second to anyone; I deserve to be first. I worked my ass off in this relationship. I've sacrificed a great deal to be with you and to make you happy," *Maya's statement infuriates me.*

"Oh, you're talking like you're the only one in this relationship? Did you forget my sacrifices and what I had to do to keep us afloat? I'm working just as hard in this relationship," *I try to remain calm.* "Maya, you're the love of my life. I'm marrying you, for God's sake. Doesn't that stand for something?" *My indiscretion has caused this tension between us. Maya isn't a fool. When Jodie's around us, Maya does not exist. She's captured my heart and all of my devotion. I would like to marry Maya, but if Jodie told me not to, I would leave Maya in a heartbeat.*

"If I'm your number one, keep your eyes where they belong and stop asking questions about her."

"I don't understand you sometimes, Maya. You asked me about her coming by here, and then you flipped on me because I asked a few questions. Don't ask me anything else about Jodie, ok? I don't want to know. She's your friend, not mine. I don't want to know anything between you and her."

"Good!" She says, snapping her fingers and heading back to the kitchen.

CHAPTER 2

JODIE:

I have second thoughts about opening up to Maya. I told her I would be there today with something essential to share. I wonder how she'll react. It's hard to hide anything from her. She knows me better than I know myself. We've been friends since college. She's like a sister to me. Maya and I attended the same high school but weren't close until we met at the University. She received her bachelor's in accounting at Johns Hopkins University, and I received my bachelor's degree in business administration. After graduation, we decided to stay near one another. I live a short distance from her in a one-bedroom condominium in Baltimore, Maryland. I love the Towers at Harbor Court, where my condo is.

The view from my window looking down into the harbor is lovely at any time of the day. Still, it is incredibly stimulating during summer when vacationers populate the harbor. I love the smell of the sea and the view of the ocean. A cool breeze is blowing through my window, lessening the current humidity. I'm just about ready to make my journey to Maya's place. I feel strange inside, and I don't have an appetite. I've thought about not telling her and postponing my visit for the past few days, but I must be honest. If I genuinely want to do this, I must come clean. She knows when I'm not telling the truth anyway. I've made my decision months ago when I started this relationship. I don't want to change how things are going in my life. I feel alive and well. Like a child with a new toy, I can't get enough of indulging in it. To think about him makes me warm with excitement. I haven't seen him in a few weeks. Nursing this calf injury and redecorating homes has me swamped.

I don't know how I will react around him when I get there. I've never done anything like this before. Maya is my girl. How did I get myself into this situation? I guess it's too late to try to change it now. My cell is ringing. It's Maya's ringtone. Should I or shouldn't I answer it? She probably wants

13

to know if I'm still coming over. It's getting late. Let me answer it and at least have a pleasant conversation with her before all hell breaks loose.

"Hello."

"Jodie, are you still coming, girl? It's almost seven. You were supposed to be here by six-thirty, remember?"

"I'm coming, Maya. I'm just running behind. It's difficult getting around with this calf injury. I have to move kind of slow."

"Oops, I forgot about that. Is it getting any better?"

"The doctor told me the only thing that can help it is a lot of rest, no jogging."

"I know you hated to hear those words."

"Yes, I did. Running is my life. I have to keep this beautiful figure in shape. I'm originally a thick woman. If I slack off just a tad bit, my ass will be all over the place. I have to keep it tight and right."

"Well, if it spreads out too much, you can give some to me. I can use a little bit more back there."

"Girl, you have a nice shape. Why do you want more junk in the trunk?"

"I need Julius's eyes staying glued to me instead of other places."

"Yeah, I guess it doesn't hurt to have a bit more assets than the rest."

"Jodie, you, of all people, should know that better than anyone else." *I detect a hint of anger in her tone, almost as if she's implying something. Maybe she knows or has some kind of idea of what's happening. No, it can't be. He would never tell her. Not without my approval first.*

"Having a lot of backside can be a blessing and a curse. Men are constantly staring at my ass. Sometimes, I just want to shrink it so they can stop looking at it. I have to be careful of what I choose to wear, with horny men running around twenty-four-seven. I even have the teenagers whistling at me. It gets very annoying sometimes like I'm live bait."

"Maybe you should stop flaunting it so much, and then they would keep their eyes to themselves or on their women instead." *Her statement is clear to me. She has to know, but how did she find out? If she had known, she would have been more upset than this. Her innuendos are beginning to tick me off.*

"I don't flaunt anything, Maya. I don't have to. All I have to do is show up, and they come running. It's natural. It's in my DNA." *Take that, Maya. I can sling shit too.*

"You must show up soon because the food is almost ready. I'm not reheating it. It doesn't taste the same when you warm it a second time. I need you to be here like yesterday."

"Are you ok, Maya? It seems like something is bothering you, girl?"

"What gives you that impression?"

"Your tone of voice is edgy."

"Edgy? Maybe I am. I just cooked all this food in this heat wave. Julius hasn't helped me at all. He's sitting in the living room next to the AC. We just argued. I hate when he lies to me."

"What is he lying about?"

"Sometimes he thinks I'm a fool. I know when he's lying and when he's telling the truth. His body language gives him away. He gets fidgety when he's not telling the truth. I can't stand a liar. Just be honest with me. I can at least respect that, but don't lie to me."

"You still haven't told me what he's lying about."

"You'll find out when you get here. Maybe you can help. He will have no choice but to tell the truth in front of you."

"I don't think that's a good idea. The two of you have built a relationship together. There's no need for an outsider to get in the middle of it. That's your man, and you're his woman."

"I couldn't agree with you more. My point exactly," *here she goes again.*

"I'm leaving the house. I'll see you when I get there."

"Call me when you're five minutes out so I can set the table."

"OK. Bye,"

I could detect tightness in her voice. Maya knows something. How much does she know? I will find out when I get there. Over the years, she has been a true friend to me. I love her like a sister, but I can't change the decision I've already made. I must go through with it. Maya has never been the violent type. I don't know how she'll respond, but I'm ready for anything. If something pops off, I have a can of pepper spray in my purse. I can't believe I'm considering harming my girl over a man. He's not just any man. J makes me crazy inside to the point of doing whatever it takes to keep him. I've never been this blindsided before over someone. Seeing him when I get there has my panties in pandemonium. Back in college, Maya and I were like partners in crime. We played on men whenever we felt it was necessary. If I was seeing someone, she considered the guy off limits and vice versa for me. We always had each other's back. It will be difficult to lose her friendship. Then again, having J by my side will make it easier. I will probably catch Hell later for being dishonest to Maya. I should have used better judgment. Let me stop. It's too late to go back. I've already committed my sin. I have to live with it.

I park my car in Maya's driveway. I turn off the engine. I have clammy hands along with a guilty heart. I think about restarting the car and taking off. This is one of the hardest and harshest things I've ever done. I hope J does most of the talking. I'm too nervous to speak. What will she do when she finds out? What will be her decision? I rechecked my purse to ensure my pepper spray was inside. I have a strong inclination I will have to use it. Maya doesn't deserve any of this. She's been there for me when things weren't going so swell. I remember just last year when I had a stalker following me. It was my fault. I led him on. I dated him for some time and then ditched him. He didn't take it very lightly. He followed me for months. I informed the police, and the police said as long as he hasn't harmed me, there's not much they can do. It's a free country. He can travel where he pleases. Everywhere I turned, there he was. It became intolerable for me.

I told Maya about it, and she helped me solve the problem. Maya has four brothers, and they know the streets reasonably well. She told them I had an issue with a guy following me around. I don't know what they did to this very day, but I've never seen this stalker anymore. Her brothers said I am family and will do anything to help me. My legs are shaky walking up to Maya's door. I wipe my hands on the sides of my black mini-skirt. I look down, checking my black Chanel sandals, making sure my French pedicure is up to par. I adjusted my white blouse by loosening the first button. I push down any hair that is out of place. I'm now ready to ring the doorbell. Before I could press the doorbell, Maya opened the door, greeting me with a smile. I feel more ashamed after seeing her face. This is so wrong. Why am I doing this to her? She doesn't deserve it.

"Girl, how long are you going to stand there? I told you to call me when you were close. The food has been ready for some time now. Come on in so we can eat. Julius and I are starving. Go sit down in the dining room. Julius is setting the table. I have to bring out the food."

"Don't you need help bringing out the food?" I try to stall.

"Jodie, take your behind in the dining room, woman. I got this. The plates and utensils are on the table. I only have to bring out the dinner."

"I have to wash my hands first."

"Ok, hurry up."

I stare at my twenty-five-year-old reflection in the bathroom mirror while washing my hands thoroughly as if trying to cleanse them from sin. I look beautiful, but I feel pitiful. My satisfying appearance cannot hide the awful feeling of dishonesty inside my soul. I heard Maya's doorbell ringing no sooner than I turned the faucet off. I dry my hands and tentatively make my way into the dining room. Julius is seated at the end of the dinner table. He's looking very handsome. His muscles are protruding through his satin short-sleeved white shirt. I can smell his cologne from across the room. He gets up from the table and pulls out my chair. I politely thanked him and sat down.

"Jodie, I need to share something with you," he says, standing over me.

"What is it?" I ask.

"I would like to know too! What do you have to share with her and not me?" Maya yells from behind us. Julius and I turn around to see Maya fuming and her brother standing beside her. She rushes over to Julius belligerently, putting her hand in his face. Julius tries to move her hand away from his face. "What do you have to tell her, Julius? I'm your fiancée. What the hell do you have to tell her and not me?" Julius is holding onto both of her hands, now inches from his face.

"Get your hands off my sister," her brother yells out.

"Well, tell her to get her hands out of my face then," Julius hollers back.

"I'm not telling her a thing. You probably deserve it. I never liked your sneaky ass from day one," Julius sidesteps Maya and heads straight for her brother.

"The feeling is mutual nigga. We can do this thing right here, right now," *Julius positions himself for a fight as Maya's brother edges in closer. An all-out brawl is about to go down. Julius and Maya's brother detest one another. They always have. Maya told me it had started well before she met Julius, which had transpired back in the day. Whatever it was, it must've been severe because it's like mixing cats and dogs in the same room. I will not sit here and allow this nonsense to proceed. Julius only wanted to tell me something. Maya's reaction was uncalled for, sparking her brother to lose his cool.*

"You guys need to stop it!" I scream out over the bickering. The three of them turned to look at me in unison like they couldn't believe what I had just said. "That's right, I just said it. Now, will the three of you try to act like civilized humans so we can sit down and eat? Maya, you said you were starved and have been waiting for a while to eat. You cooked all this food, and Julius set the table. Can we please eat and cut out the drama? I didn't drive over here for this," Maya's piercing eyes turn away from Julius. She stares at me for a few seconds. Then she turns to her brother, placing a hand on his shoulder.

"She's right, let's eat. What's done in the dark shall come to light anyway," she sarcastically says, storming out of the dining room. Her brother follows behind her heels to the kitchen. Julius has this weird expression on his face. Whatever he wanted to tell me before Maya interrupted, he didn't mention it again or even look in my direction. Maya and her brother returned from the kitchen with food in hand and placed it on the table. Maya says grace, and we begin serving ourselves.

"So Jodie, we're all here for your announcement. I organized this gathering specifically for you. I'm ready for what you have to tell us. That's if there aren't any more interruptions, I presume?" She cuts her eyes on Julius and then back to me. Julius ignores her comment and continues eating dinner without lifting his head. "I assume we're ready then." *My day has finally arrived. At first, I was nervous and fearful about opening up to Maya concerning J and me. But how I look at it, I deserve to be happy too. She needs to know she can't control everything in life. Certain things have to happen, and it's how the world operates. We can't have it all. She has more than enough already. Her demanding attitude is starting to irk me. I don't know who she thinks she is. Everyone at the table has stopped eating. J raised his head and stared in my direction. Instead of watching me, Maya glued her eyes on J. Her brother was very interested in what I said.*

"Maya, I don't know how you will take this. We've been friends for a while. You will probably think my worst when it's all said and done. To tell you the truth, I don't care," her mouth drops open.

"What are you trying to say, Jodie? This better not be what I think it is. So help me, God, it better not be what I think it is," she says, scanning me and Julius.

"Let her talk, Maya. I want to hear this too," her brother interjects. Maya gives in for the moment.

"Jeffrey and I are getting engaged," Maya stands up from the table, fuming.

"Jeffrey, is this true?" She asks her brother.

"It's true, Maya. We've been dating for some time. We just didn't know how to tell you without upsetting you."

"You're damn right! I don't care how you sugarcoat it. I will not accept it. Jodie, how can you date my brother? I told you never to have a relationship with any of my brothers; they're off-limits to you," she yells.

"What's the big issue, Maya? We love each other. How can you not accept it?"

"Because you're not fit for my brother. He deserves better."

CHAPTER 3

MAYA

After washing the never-ending flow of dishes in the sink, I sit at the kitchen table, exhausted. My lasagna came out perfect—just the way my mother makes it. I was the only one at the table eating it. All of that work for nothing. The cooking and cleaning up afterward has me worn out mentally and physically. Julius didn't even offer to help me. He stormed out of there as soon as Jodie and Jeffrey announced. I threw the two of them out after he left. His actions surprised me, considering I should be the one upset. Lately, Julius he's been acting very odd. He says he doesn't desire Jodie, but what did he say to her privately? I need to know. I also need to understand why Jodie decided to date my brother. We made a promise never to date family members, especially with Jodie's sexual past in question.

n college, Jodie screwed everything in sight. She used her God-given elements to lure half the male student body. She bragged frequently to me about her conquests. I had to work on campus to have money after spending my excess financial aid. I was one of the broke students living on campus.

On the other hand, Jodie had a stash of cash that never diminished. She pursued the men whose parents had money. Jodie never spent a dime of her own money. She made the men with the least amount of cash wear condoms. If their parents were well off, she let them enter her without protection. She allowed them to feel the warmth inside of her. They would give her anything in return. Diseases by no means deterred her transgressions.

The thought of Jodie and Jeffrey getting married upsets me entirely. How in God's name can Jodie go after my brother? When did it happen? And why wasn't I aware of it? If Jeffrey knew what was good for him, he would run for the border and never turn back. My thoughts are interrupted when Julius opens the front door. I get up from the table, heading for the living room.

"Woman, don't start with me. I'm not in the mood to argue."

"Julius, why did you walk out? You just left here without saying a word to me. How do you think that made me feel? My girlfriend has betrayed me, and my fiancée doesn't give a damn about my feelings."

"I left out of here because I didn't want to hear you arguing back and forth with Jodie and your brother. You can't control everything, Maya. That's your biggest fault. Why do you constantly need to have control?"

"I don't always need to have control. I just know when I'm right, and this is very wrong to me. I will not allow this relationship to continue. Mark my words on that."

"The two of them are adults. They can be with whoever they choose. I don't think they need your approval. You are going too far with this. I can't believe the way you acted. How can you treat your girlfriend like that?" *I can't believe he has the nerve to take her side after what she's done to me. He's probably sleeping with her too. Why do men fall all over her? I'm just sick of it.*

"It would take me the rest of the night to explain," he gives me a puzzling look.

"I get it now. It's okay to be friends with her, but is it not okay for her to be with your brother? Then you were never a true friend at all."

"How dare you say that to me? I will always be her friend. In the same way, I will always be an aunt, sister, and maybe someday a wife. But wrong is wrong. When I did wrong things as a child, my mother and father punished me for it. It doesn't mean they stopped loving me."

"Here we go again, back to the control issue. You are not their parents. Let it go already." *I will not let it go. They will feel my wrath.*

"Julius, you don't have the faintest idea about respect. She disrespected me. The same way you're disrespecting me at the moment.

I thought you would have my back on this, but I see you're too focused on her ass like everyone else."

"My focus is on you."

"Then prove it to me. Be honest with me."

"I am being honest," he says, grabbing me by the hand.

"Not true."

"What isn't true?"

"The way you look at Jodie."

"I'm not the one head over hills for Jodie. It's your brother. Did you see how he looked at her at the table?"

"It's you too."

"Are you implying I want her?"

"You tell me? Is there something else I should know about, like the thing you had to tell her? What did you have to tell her while I was in the kitchen? She has your undivided attention without even trying. And trust me, I know when she's trying," he lets go of my hand.

"You need to stop this, Maya. I love you and only you. There's no Jodie in the picture. I wanted to show Jodie the wedding ban I purchased for you. It was meant to be a surprise. Your jealousy just ruined it." *I don't know what to say. He's been planning this wedding since last year, even working extra hours. When he proposed to me, I had a difficult time believing it. Julius is the handsomest man I have ever seen. I know there are probably better-looking people there, but lord, this man is so fine. I'm talking about the kind of fine where you forget your name when introducing yourself. When he approached me the very first time, I almost forgot my name. I was so embarrassed. I didn't think a man like Julius would ever be interested in a woman like me. I'm not chopped liver either. I can make heads turn on any given day, but when you see a man with Julius's qualities you just assume one of those cover girl models should be draped around his arm.*

"Forgive me, J. I've let my imagination run wild lately. Part of it stems from the lack of attention you've been showing me. When was the last time you made love to me? Or the last time you brought me flowers and a dozen red-stemmed roses? In the beginning, you were Mr. Romantic. You did these things quite often. Now, you barely kiss me good night before you go to bed if I don't ask you to. Sometimes, I feel alone in your company, and a fiancé shouldn't feel this way. I need to know if I'm still your main focus."

"Baby, look, I've been running around like crazy trying to put the finishing touches on this wedding. If I have unintentionally neglected you, I'm sorry for that. I want this wedding to be awesome. You mean the world to me, and I would like everyone to know exactly how I feel about you."

"It doesn't seem that way when Jodie's around us."

"I give up talking about this. It's useless trying to get through to you."

"Maybe I should give up too," his mouth drops.

"Give up what?" *I need to think clearly before I say something I might regret later. Words can hurt. I still love Julius very much. We're getting married in a month.*

"I need to give up this talk for now. Besides, I'm exhausted, and I need to lie down."

"Can I lay down with you?" *I see; now that you're horny, you want to pay me some attention. I don't need that kind of attention. I need emotional support and a man that understands me, not just my vagina. I'll fix your ass tonight. You won't be getting any of this tonight. You better use your hand and fantasize about it.*

"I'm not in the mood, J. I cooked without your help, and I cleaned up all the dishes that were in the sink. It's time for me to relax. You can rub my feet if you would like to. They hurt from standing up all day." *Julius has a foot fetish. I know this will drive him over the edge. He loves my perfect toes and the smooth curvature of my feet, mainly when polished in his favorite co, Lore Purple Passio, as they are right now. He hesitates to respond, knowing he will be in for a battle to offset his desire.*

"I'll rub them for you," the words barely escape his lips. *I smile at him. I will tease him and give him nothing in return.*

The next day, I sit behind my desk, checking my watch occasionally. Time can't pass by quickly enough for me. My secretary buzzes me through the intercom.

"Yes, Gertrude, what is it?" I politely ask.

"I have a fresh pot of brewed coffee. Would you like me to bring you a cup?"

"Gertrude, nice timing. I will take your offer. Maybe some fresh coffee can put me back on track. My mother always seems to think so," Gertrude walks inside my office, places the black coffee mug on my desk, and turns to walk out.

"Gertrude, have a seat. And besides, I need to take a little break. These numbers are beating my behind."

"Is it something I can help you with?" *Maybe Gertrude can help me. She's very resourceful. Gertrude has attended law school but could never pass the bar exam. She worked as a paralegal for many years until the realization that she would not ever be able to practice law set in. Her secretarial skills are stellar.*

"For my life, I can't find out where certain funds are going. I've checked my books over and over and have been unsuccessful. The loans we have issued are accruing interest, and the payments are up to date, but there are thousands of dollars going out unaccounted for," Gertrude frowns, causing a line to appear across her forehead. She stares at me attentively.

"Ms. M, did you know that Thomas handles many of the sizable accounts?"

"Mr. Pearson's nephew?"

"Yes, he puts his final stamp on a loan if he thinks it's legitimate."

"When did this happen?"

"I think it happened when Mr. Pearson was diagnosed with Alzheimer's disease. His memory is starting to fail him. Since he doesn't have any children, he decided to groom Thomas in the workings of the company, which he will later on be his uncle's successor, the CEO of H&L Holdings. He may be able to help you with your problem."

"Gertrude, thanks for the heads up. I owe you one."

"No problem, that's what I'm here for." *Gertrude is amazing. She would make a great lawyer.*

I create an entry in my ledger, checking thoroughly to ensure my calculations are precise. I work for one of the largest mortgage companies in Baltimore. H&L Holdings owns half the property in the city of Baltimore. The company is ranked 54 out of the top 100 mortgage lenders. H&L has 25 locations in Maryland, Virginia, Pennsylvania, New Jersey, North Carolina, Indiana, Ohio, and Illinois. Its corporate office is here in Baltimore. They have closed roughly 35,000 loans to date. In 2014, their annual volume was approximately one billion dollars. I am blessed to have this position. I do pretty well for myself. They treat me like a partner of the company. I don't have any complaints. I love where I work, but my numbers haven't increased lately. I've recalculated my numbers, and I'm finding my calculations now are in the red. The Jodie and Jeffrey situation has me in a rut. I must refocus on my job before they throw me out the door. I can't get the two of them out of my head. I will do everything in my power to break them apart. But first things first, I have to give Thomas a call and balance this ledger.

CHAPTER 4

JEFFREY:

I don't know what the big fuss is about. Maya must accept it because Jodie and I aren't going anywhere. Our relationship is here to stay. I told her I love Jodie, and I genuinely mean that. She should be thrilled her baby brother and girlfriend is an item. Jodie is keeping it in the family; one day, we will have children to expand our family. I love Jodie more than life itself. How could I ever survive without her? She's the epitome of a real woman. It doesn't even bother me when people stare at us in public. I find it amusing when it happens, which is so predictable of them. f the bold ones have gone out of their way to express their discontent against our interracial pairing. This past summer at the festival in the Harbor, a Caucasian male dared to ask Jodie why she doesn't stick with her kind. I was enraged by his comment until Jodie calmed me down. I'm learning to brush off the insults and constant stares as time progresses. She has received her share of offenses as well. Black women get downright incensed when they see us together. Once, we were in the grocery store, and an elderly black woman told Jodie that her race needed to stop taking all the good black men away. The senior citizen wanted to fight Jodie in the store's produce section. It was one of the craziest things I ever witnessed. The thought of apples and oranges flying around was hilarious to me. If these incidents haven't separated us yet, then Maya's disapproval doesn't stand a chance. We're together for the long haul.

It's been a week since we made our announcement, and Maya hasn't spoken two words to us. I find it baffling. My brothers are happy for me. I think there is a little envy of me. Jodie is the type of woman who can stand in a crowd of other women and get noticed by men. Men can't seem to keep their eyes off of her. It doesn't matter what she's wearing, or if her hair is unprepared, men lose control. Sometimes it bothers me when their eyes stick to her ass. But like I stated before, I'm learning how to handle the negative attention. I know my woman is sexy. The world thinks it, too.

She's mine and only belongs to me. I refuse to share her with anyone else. They can look all they want as long as they don't touch.

"Jeffrey, you know I love you, right?" She asks, smiling at me, showing her pearly whites and wearing nothing but silk panties in our bedroom.

"And I love you back, even more than you love me."

"Are you sure Maya didn't scare you away? I take a deep breath, slowly exhaling.

"I love my sister just as much as I love you, although I will not let her dictate my life. It's her fault anyway. She gets all the blame."

"How do you figure that?"

"Remember when that guy was stalking you?"

"How can I forget? He scared me half to death."

"When you asked Maya to help you, we took care of it."

"I am honestly thankful for that. By the way, what did you guys do to him?"

"Just put it this way: you will never have to worry about him again."

"So, that's how you fell for me?"

"Yes, honey. All of us did, but my brothers were married. I was the only single one in the group. They told me to talk to you and try it," her probing green eyes examine me.

"You honestly thought you were all that, didn't you?" she teases.

"I pulled you in, didn't I?"

"You sure did. How could I resist your clean-shaven head and beautiful brown eyes?" She seductively rubs her tongue over her top lip. Come here, baby, so that I can feel your bald head.

"Is that all you want to feel?"

"No, I want to touch and feel everything."

After Jodie and I made love to each other which felt like an eternity, we were undeniably ready for bed. Jodie keeps me aroused for hours at a time. Her sex drive is voracious. She's constantly trying new things and buying different toys to spark our relationship. She's like a sex goddess to me. There's times when I want to end our carnal adventures from being so exhausted. I won't give in though. I have to satisfy her. It's my job as her man to give her what she needs. I will not let anyone else have Jodie due to my incapability of pleasing her. The notion of another man even touching her is something I wouldn't be able to handle. I guess it's why my thoughts are on Julius as I look at Jodie lying next to me. It's odd how he left the room when Jodie and I made our announcement. He stormed out of there like he was hurt. Whatever he was trying to hide from Maya he certainly can't hide it from me. I saw the pain in his eyes. He has feelings for Jodie. I'm sure he does. I wonder if Jodie recognizes it. She would have to be blind not to.

"Baby, why are you looking at me like that? Is something wrong?" She rubs her hand over my bare chest.

"Something feels wrong. It's kind of bothering me. I've been thinking about it for a while."

"What's bothering you, honey?" She asks sitting up in bed.

"It's Julius. Did you see how he stormed out of the apartment when we made our announcement? He blew his top. He acted like you were his woman or something. Didn't that seem odd to you?"

"No. Why would Julius act like that? He has your sister, and they will marry in a couple of weeks. Julius loves Maya. I see how they look at each other. They have something real special."

"I see the way he looks at you too. He tries to downplay it, but his eyes are always on you. Even before we made our announcement I've seen him in action. He can't stop looking at you."

"I don't know what to say Jeffrey. I'm definitely not attracted to him. I have you in my life. Maybe you think he feels that way, I'm positive he doesn't. Why would he be after me? It just doesn't make any sense at all."

"It makes perfect sense to me. I'm a man, and I can read between the lines. Have you ever flirted with him?" Jodie becomes irate from my question. She picks up her pillow and whacks me across the face with it."

"How can you ask me something like that? You of all people should know the answer. I would never ever disrespect my friend by talking to her man or you for that matter. It's not who I am. I can't believe you Jeffrey. You just spoiled our night," she turns her back to me in the bed. *I should've never brought it up. It was wrong for me to suggest that she had something to do with his behavior.*

"Jodie, I didn't mean that. I don't know what's wrong with me. I'm so overly attached to you that I sometimes get jealous. I'm sorry baby. I just love you so damn much. Can you forgive me?" Jodie turns back over and just stares at me without saying a word.

"Baby listen, I didn't mean it. I'm sorry for suggesting it. Can you please say something to me?"

"Something," she laughs out loud. I laugh along with her, giving her a bear hug. "Jeffrey, you need to realize that I'm your woman. I'm not going anywhere, and you also need to understand that men will be men. Men constantly look at women. You're a man. You've looked at other women, and you probably still do. It's prewired in our DNA to be attracted to the opposite sex. It doesn't mean because we look we have to touch. It's just a little reminder that we're desired and someone thinks were attractive. It's only attention. We don't have to act upon it. You tell me I'm "hot" all the time. If you think this way about me others probably feel the same, unless you're lying to me?"

"Jodie, you drive me crazy with your fine ass. I don't want to share you with anyone," she smiles at me.

"You don't have to because I'm all yours," she kisses me firmly on the lips. "Goodnight Jeffrey, I love you."

"Goodnight Jodie, I love you too."

CHAPTER 5

JULIUS

It's been two weeks since I witnessed the spectacle that took place in our apartment. How can Jodie play me like this? We were just in a hotel room a month ago experiencing sensual pleasure to the highest level. How in the world can she be engaged to this cornball? She's never mentioned Jeffrey's name not once to me. I should've shaken the hell out of her when she made the announcement in front of us. If Maya wasn't around I probably would have. I'm so enraged. I can't focus on anything else but Jodie's betrayal. Has she lost her fucking mind? As bad as I feel for what she's done to me, I continue to crave her like a drug addict needing a fix. I know I'm wrong to judge her considering what I'm doing to Maya, but I thought we understood each other. Jodie told me she was falling in love with me and wanted to bring our affair to a more meaningful level. I feel the same as her. I assumed down the line we would turn our affair into legitimacy. This has caught me by surprise. I'm definitely in shock. She makes love to me like I'm the last man standing, and the next time I see her she's with Maya's brother. To sit there and listen to their plans on getting married certainly has taken its toll on me. I didn't have the slightest clue that Jeffrey was seeing her. Even now, it's hard for me to comprehend.

Then again, I wasn't with her every moment of the day. I have a fiancé to attend to. Maybe she started seeing Jeffrey because of the time I spent with Maya. My hands are tied, and I'm sure she resents me for it. She protested to me often. I never thought she would take it to this point of revenge. I can't tolerate the idea of the two of them together. I feel worse than Maya, and for good reason. On the flip side, I probably deserve this for treating Maya like garbage. Perhaps I should steer my focus on Maya and formulate this marriage thing once and for all. Maya isn't a bad woman. She's undeniably beautiful, and I am lucky to have her. I need to start treating her like it. Suppose Jodie wants to play games with me by ignoring me like I don't exist. I can play the same game. It probably wouldn't hurt as much if she was seeing someone else. To say I hate Maya's brother with a passion is putting it mildly. He walks around with this pompous attitude like he's better than everyone else. When I'd known him, Jodie was the fourth white girl he'd dated. He dates nothing but white women and associates exclusively with Caucasians. The only black thing on that brother is his skin color; he's a straight-up sellout.

When Maya introduced me to her family, I received a warm welcome from everyone except Jeffrey. Her brothers Mike, Kyle, and Travis clicked with me right away. I grew up in the hood, and her brothers grew up in the same environment. We understood the hidden code of the streets, so we immediately bonded. On the other hand, Jeffrey acted like I wasn't good enough for his sister. He didn't shake my hand the first time I met him and refused to look me in the face. He wanted her to be with some Ivy League dude, preferably white. Her mother and father were excited to meet me. They reminded me of my parents. Her parents believe in family cohesiveness and include their children in everything. Her father is a pastor at a church in the area. From here on out, I will devote more time to Maya. I will make our wedding a day to remember. I'll make sure to invite Jeffrey and Jodie despite Maya's unwillingness. No woman is going to use me and expect me to roll over. She's only a piece of meat to me anyway. Why cry over a hamburger when I have steak at home? Jodie planned to do this to me. I know it. I'm sure she's done this before to other men. How were they able to cope; only God knows.

"Bus driver, you missed my stop! What's wrong with you? Don't you know how to do your job? The elderly black woman yells from the rear of the bus as I try to refocus on my route. I unintentionally drove past her stop with my thoughts concerning Jodie.

"Ms. I'm very sorry. My mind was somewhere else," I explain to her while stopping halfway past her bus stop.

"I'm too old to be walking this distance, and it's hot out there. I have all these bags in my hand to carry. I didn't pay my bus fare for this kind of service," I remain quiet as the elderly woman approaches the side door to exit the bus. "If you can't perform your job correctly you shouldn't do it at all," she walks down the stairs.

"Mam, I will help you carry them. That's if the bus driver waits for me," Benny teasingly says sitting directly behind me.

"He had better wait for you. It's his fault, anyway. It's the least he can do," I tell Benny to help her, and I will wait for him. *I announce to the other passengers who don't look too happy, that I'm sorry for their inconvenience. If there was a way to change the mistakes in my life I wouldn't be behind the wheel of this city bus driving in an area that I loathe. Crenshaw Avenue is one of the worst areas in the city of Baltimore. This area has with panhandlers, beggars, thieves, con artists, prostitutes, and the homeless, all of which ride this bus. On any given day of the week, something terrible is constantly occurring. The worst of the worst live in this small, congested county. Benny returns to the bus and sits behind me as usual.*

"What's going on J, you never miss a stop? I ride this loud bus five times a week and I've never seen you forget a stop. Out of all the people that ride this bus you had to choose her stop to miss. The minute she stepped on this bus I knew she was a problem."

"How could you tell that? She looked fine to me."

"It was obvious J. She had that kind of look that said, DON'T F WITH ME TODAY."

"Women are very complex individuals. When you think you figured one out they turn around and do the unthinkable. It's like trying to pin the tail on the donkey. Women are always on the move and three steps ahead of us while were running around in circles."

"I thought you had Maya figured out by now to be getting married to her?"

"Benny, you never really know a woman, even when you lay in the same bed with them."

"Maybe you're just not ready for marriage. I see how the women boarding this bus look at you," Benny laughs.

"Yeah, I guess I can't complain about the attention."

"That's the truth."

"When Maya came along I started ignoring the looks I was getting. I wanted something more meaningful in a woman."

"I would do anything to have one of those dazzling-looking women drooling over me. They won't even look in my direction like I'm transparent."

"Benny, you're not missing anything, believe me when I say it." *Benny Johnson is one of my regular passengers; most of the time we strike up conversations relating to everything. It sort of makes my day go by faster considering he's usually the last person to get off the bus. He's met Maya a few times on the bus and has recently joined our church. He loves to talk, and his mouth never stops going. I don't mind though, Benny doesn't have too many friends. He's sort of a loner. Most of his family lives in Florida. He's not married and doesn't have any children or a girlfriend. I guess his social time is when he gets on the bus to talk to me.*

"I'm missing a lot and you know it just as well as I do. I'm twenty-nine years old. I should have someone in my life by now. I thought maybe by my thirtieth birthday I would at least have a girlfriend. It's depressing being this lonely."

"Benny, when I was single I enjoyed my life. I was able to do anything and everything I wanted on my own terms. If I wanted to stay in bed half the day, I could. If I wanted to hang out at the club through the night, I could. There was no one to report to. I didn't have to check in with anyone. My schedule belonged to me. I didn't have to worry about hurting anyone's feelings. Sometimes I miss that life, especially during the bad times."

"Can we trade places then? I can go home to Maya, and you can have my dull life. I think you have the perfect wife. Everyone loves her at the church. No disrespect, but she's a head turner."

"One week with Maya and you wouldn't hesitate returning to your dull life as you say."

"Is she that bad, J?"

"She isn't all that bad. It's the little things going on right now in our relationship. We have some issues to iron out."

"Like what?

"I rather not say at this time."

"Don't forget about my baptism this Sunday. I'm finally joining the other saints."

"Congratulations Benny! I almost forgot. Sunday is your big day, and the thing about joining the other saints is overrated. There's not one saint in that church, maybe sinners, but definitely not any saints. You will fit in perfect, probably better than the rest of them."

"J, do you see that women up ahead at the bus stop?" *I see the woman very clearly, and I expect everyone else on the bus does to. How can they miss a white woman standing in the heart of the ghetto wearing a tight red mini skirt and a skimpy top leaving nothing to the imagination? I don't want to stop the bus, but there's other passengers waiting at the stop as well.*

"Yeah, I see her Benny."

"J, she must be on somethin' to be standing in the middle of the hood dressed like that. Look at all those guys standing behind her. Everybody's checking her out." *Unfortunately for me, I have to stop the bus and pick up Jodie with part of her ass hanging out in the street. She's doing this to get a reaction out of me, but I won't give her one. I refuse to give in to her sick games. If she wants to stand on the Ave and look like a whore it's alright with me.*

"She's definitely on something; it must be a new drug." *When I stop to open the service door to let her inside nearly every male passenger remaining on the bus is transfixed by her splendor. Jodie prances up the steps and takes a seat behind me. She crosses her legs causing Benny to salivate.*

"Hello handsome. I didn't think you were going to stop the bus for a minute there."

"I didn't want to, but there were other passengers at the stop as well. I couldn't just leave them."

"Oh, so I assuming if I were the only passenger you would've left me?"

"Exactly," Benny's eyes widen.

"There's so much hostility in your voice. Where is this coming from?" Her question causes me to swerve over the yellow line a bit.

"Where is my hostility coming from? Have you lost your freaking mind woman? You pull that stunt and expect me to be calm? How am I supposed to react?" She bats her eyes at Benny sticking out her hand.

"Hi there, I'm Jodie. It's nice to meet you."

"I'm Benny, nice to meet you too."

"I had to look out for me. How do you think it makes me feel when you're with Maya most of the time? I have feelings and needs, and Jeffrey has met some of those needs," *I glance at Benny in the mirror. He looks confused. I hope Benny is not taking in too much. And if he is, he'd better keep his mouth sealed.*

"Don't bring up that fool's name on my bus. Jeffrey is nothing compared to me."

"I beg to differ. He does have money and a big house."

"If he has so much shit, why are you here talking to me now? Why aren't you in his big house spending his big money?"

"I miss you, J, and I wanted to see you again," *I'm incensed by her words.*

"Woman, get the hell away from me. I don't want to have anything to do with you," I stop the bus and open the service door. She giggles lightheartedly.

"Are you sure about this? No one gets rid of me that easy," she stands up pulling down her skirt. She shakes Benny's hand one more time. "Bye handsome," she struts down the steps for everyone to see. I pull off from the curb not even giving her a second glance.

"J, are you ok?"

"Not now Benny. I have to focus on the road."

"Well, I guess my stop is up ahead. I'll see you tomorrow."

"Enjoy your day, Benny."

"I most certainly will. Try to enjoy yours."

"Ok."

CHAPTER 6

JODIE

Maya's nerve to tell me that I'm not fit for her brother is distressing. I thought she would be disappointed and eventually get over it. Her pigheadedness has no end, and she has ignored my attempts to reach her. I understand Jeffrey is her baby brother and wants to protect him from harm, but she is taking this too far. He's a man capable of making his own decisions in life. Jeffrey and I will meet with his parents today to share our news. We've told everyone except them. Jeffrey is nervous, as usual. I told him to be himself and his parents would respect that. He said his father probably would be ok with it, but his mother is unpredictable. His mother has a particular dislike for Caucasians, and she doesn't hold back her tongue. She speaks her mind. Jeffrey claims his mother has been instrumental in the riots in Baltimore concerning police brutality. Jeffrey has said he thinks the white girls he dated in the past left him because of his mother's discrimination. Jeffrey has attended white schools most of his life. He's more comfortable around white people than his own. He loves to listen to pop, rock, and even some heavy metal music. Jeffrey detests rap music and very seldom listens to R&B. I'm not the type of white girl he's used to. I like hip-hop, R&B, and reggae music. I tell him often that I'm a black girl trapped in a white body. He attended white schools, and I attended all black schools. Sometimes he acts whiter than me. I try to steer him to where his roots are, but he won't have any of it. He loves who he is, except his skin color. He hates the fact that he is a dark skinned man. I love his midnight complexion, but he detests it.

"Sugar plum; are you ready to hit the road?" Jeffrey asks.

"I'm as ready as I will ever be. The question is, are you ready?"

"I'm ready to face the challenge. I hope my mother is in a terrific mood."

"Why wouldn't she be honey?"

"I honestly wish I could answer your question, but my mother is hard to figure out sometimes. Her facial expressions don't go along with her mood. If she looks happy she's angry. If she looks angry she's happy. While growing up in our household neither of us siblings could tell the difference. It was frustrating at times."

"I'm confident she will be ok. What parent wouldn't be happy with the announcement of their son getting married?

"My mother, the Mrs. Honorable Farrakhan, that's who."

"Is she that bad when it comes to race?"

"You have no idea."

"She treated me fairly when Maya brought me over to see her."

"That's because you weren't dating one of her sons."

"I don't believe that for one bit. Your mother likes me."

"Ok, you'll see. Don't say I didn't warn you first."

I'm having a hard time coming to grips with Jeffrey's mother being a racist. I've known her since Maya and I were roommates. She's never displayed any disapproval towards me. I've been in her home several times and have eaten dinner with Maya's mother and father. They speak to me like one of their children. If Jeffrey's mother treats me unfavorably today, I will be just as hurt as J. I'm reallorried though, because I know she likes me. When we reach his parent's church Jeffrey jumps out of the car forgetting to open my door. I lightly tap the horn to his white Mercedes. He turns around sprinting to my door. He never fails to open my door. I realize his mind is occupied.

"Jodie, I'm sorry, honey. I can't believe I forgot to open your door."

"I warned you once you started you wouldn't be able to do it all the time. It's alright though J; I know the real reason behind it. This time I forgive you, but don't let it happen again," I tease him. It's like he doesn't even hear me. He is so focused on his mother. I softly touch his face and rub my hand over his shaven head. "Everything will be fine. Trust me. You're worrying too much. J, take a deep breath. Hold it for a couple of seconds. Now, let it out. Is that better?" *He tells me it is. From the look on his face I don't believe him.*

"I just want my mother to approve of you. I love you more than words can say. I don't know what I would do without you."

"I love you the same J. Now, let's get moving. We have an announcement to make."

Shiloh Baptist Church isn't the biggest church in the city of Baltimore. By many, it's considered one of the most influential churches in the area—the church seats just over a thousand congregants. Membership is steady, and everyone in Jeffrey's family helps to keep it running smoothly. It stands suitably on the corner of West and Third Street, easily accessible to the public. Jeffrey's father planned the architectural layout of the building. The church's scheme looks like a giant cross if viewing it from above. As Jeffrey and I make our way through the double doors, I prepare myself for the unexpected. We bypassed the atrium and walked inside the sanctuary, where J's father stood beside J's mother behind the podium. Why are they behind the podium instead of greeting us? I would like to know. His father speaks into the microphone, prompting us to sit down. I sit down with J. I'm nervous, not knowing what to expect. I don't know whether to keep my hands folded or to put them on my lap. J fidgets with his keys. I place my hand overhims so he can stop.

"I would like to start with a brief sermon about love. I wrote it last night after Maya informed me of your decision." *The nerve of her to upstage our moment, how petty.* "So, listen very carefully. First and foremost, keep God in your life. And put him first before all things. Pray for him to look over you in all that you do. Ask for his blessings and his guidance. Son and soon-to-be-daughter-in-law, I realize your love for one another is tremendous. Love is a beautiful thing, and it can also turn ugly. First, I will talk about the beauty of love. When we first set eyes on that person, we consider our soulmate; it's like no other feeling imaginable. Money and riches cannot replace it, and there's never enough time in the day to spend with each other. The joy of seeing their smile and the pleasure of knowing this person loves you the same way you love them is incredible. The joy of creating a child in the image of you both is remarkable. The two of you become one instead of two. Before you can finish your sentence, they finish it for you. Some of your dislikes become likes as you complement one another through love. Your heartbeat flutters every time you think about each other. This love, this compelling emotion, is beautiful when it's working. But when it's not, it can be dangerous. Son and my soon-to-be daughter-in-law, you must trust one another to keep your love intact. Without it, your love will surely die.

Today, forty to fifty percent of all marriages end in divorce. The reasons to blame can be several. It stems from a lack of trust, commitment, and communication. It is vital in a marriage that you can rely on the other person. In times of struggle, you have to believe they have your back and are willing to do everything they can to support you when hard times unravel you. A committed couple is a blessed couple. Vowing to stay faithful in your marriage will lessen the temptations that wait around every corner. Satan travels to and fro. His job is to deceive you in any form possible. Lust, fornication, and adultery are his prime characteristics. The battle with him will be impossible without commitment and keeping God's word close to your heart. A successful relationship depends on communication.

Talking with each other and sharing your thoughts and disagreements can assist you in growing more robust as a couple. Being on the same page when adversity strikes helps us to counteract any present danger." After finishing his brief sermon, J's father had a big smile. His mother's expression hasn't changed since we sat down. Her lips drawnn n, and her eyes pronounce contempt. I don't know if she's happy for us, or in shock. His father steps away from the podium as his mother takes his place. She looks at me as if she's trying to see through me. I feel uncomfortable. I turn to J for support. He doesn't even look my way. He looks petrified.

"Honey, are you sure this is what you want? Now before you answer me, just think about it for a moment. You're about to make a lifetime decision. Getting married is a serious thing. It's not child's play, and matrimony is more than just skin deep." *I can't believe what she just said. Is she referring to my ethnicity? Is she saying this because I'm white?* Jeffrey, your father and I want the best for you. We always have. I think you're rushing into things. How long have you known this woman anyway? Excuse me, I'm so sorry, I mean Jodie." *She just called me this woman? Who the hell does she think she is? Someone needs to check her. J's father just stands there with his head down. They're both afraid of her, but I'm not. If she continues to degrade me in this fashion I will show her what I'm made of.*

"We've dated for about a year, and we love each other exclusively. I'm sure of it. I've never felt this way about anyone," *she looks me up and down in distaste, and then turns back to her son.*

"A year is not enough time to get to know a person. In the early stages we put on our best face to attract the one we want. Our real face doesn't appear until later or when it's too late. Do you know everything about her?" *Her? What am I, a stranger off the street? J needs to stand up for me. I'm his fiancée. If he's going to be my husband he had better pull his pants up and be a man. She has a sickening smirk on her face I would like to remove permanently with both my hands.*

"Mom, her name is Jodie. Can you please call her by her name?"

"Don't you dare correct me? I know exactly what her name is," *she glares at me, and I crack a light smile of satisfaction.*

"I know everything I need to know about her right now. And that's just it. I want to acquire more about her as time goes on. I want to be challenged. I want to be surprised when she does special things out of the norm. I want the spark to keep going and never fade away."

"Boy, what kind of craziness are you talking about? Do you know that you sound like a child? Only children make decisions without thinking them through. Do you really know everything there is to know about this woman?" J jumps up from his seat in an animated fashion.

"Ma, if you can't call her by her name I will not sit through this any longer. It's not right. She hasn't done anything at all to be disrespected like this. She's going to be my wife whether you like it or not."

"He's right honey. You need to call her by her name, enough is enough?" *His father actually says something. They're finally acting like men and not cowards. I'm so proud of J for standing up to her. She sucks her teeth giving her husband a perturbed expression.*

"Jodie, if I offended you in any way, I apologize. I just want the best for my son." *I don't believe you.*

"How much do you really know about Jodie?"

"I know enough to marry her."

"Son, don't be forced into doing something you don't want to. If she's pressuring you to marry her then it really isn't love." *Pressuring him? Why would I pressure him? He proposed to me and I accepted.*

"Mom and dad, I came here for your support and not to be judged. I will marry Jodie no matter what anyone says or thinks. It's already in the works. Nothing is going to stop us. On that note, Jodie and I have other important matters to attend to. Our wedding date will be sometime next year. I will keep you posted. Good day mom and good day dad. J reaches for my hand. I desperately grab his in search of the exit. I turn back to look at his parents. His father is beaming from ear to ear. He seems to be fighting to hold back his excitement for J. His mother on the other hand has a poker face on. It's difficult for me to read her.

CHAPTER 7

MAYA

"I can't believe that boy."

"Mom, why is it so hard to believe? He's been with nothing but white girls his whole life."

"I thought he would grow out of it by now. You know, like a fad or a played out style."

"Mom, these are women you're talking about, not clothing. He's into them. The sad part is I don't think he knows anything else."

"Has he ever been with a black girl?"

"C'mon mom, were talking about Jeffrey. He doesn't travel on the dark side."

"But, he's dark himself."

"His dark complexion doesn't correlate with him dating dark skinned women. He's a regular OJ Simpson."

"I hope he doesn't turn out like OJ. I need my son to be here, not in some prison rotting away because of a white woman."

"It upsets me too. Jodie knew better than to date Jeffrey. They hid it from me. I told her not to go there, and she went there anyway."

"What do you really know about her?"

"She's promiscuous. Back in college, she had her share of men. I don't know if she's still the same, but you never know these days. Everyone is having sex with everyone."

"My son is about to marry a whore? I will not allow it. This must be prevented. How did you let this happen?" *Is she serious? Jeffrey is a man. He makes his own decisions.*

"First of all, Jeffrey is a man. He makes his own decisions. I can't tell him what to do. Those days of me being the older sister with the motherly advice are over. Mom, Jodie can draw attention from anywhere. Men seem to fall all over her. They can't resist her."

"She is beautiful Maya. I can't deny that, although she's not the only pretty woman out there. We need to find someone that can hold a candle to her."

"Mom, what are you saying?"

"You know exactly what I'm saying. We have to find someone that can knock his socks off, and he will eventually forget about Jodie." *I can't believe what my mother is suggesting.*

"Mom, you're the first lady of Shiloh Baptist Church and the assistant pastor. This will look bad if anyone finds out. Dad will throw a fit if he discovers this."

"Oh, don't you worry about MR. Bible. I have your father wrapped around my finger. And besides, he will never find out. This is between you and me."

"If I decide to help you do this, where do we find a woman to upstage Jodie and pull Jeffrey away from her?"

"A call girl." *Has she lost her mind? My mother will go to any means necessary to protect her sons.*

"A prostitute?

"A call girl is different than a prostitute. They're classy and stylish, and much more beautiful. *I'm not fond of her proposition.*

"Mom, were taking a huge risk. The people in this community respect us. We do so much to encourage their lives. If this were to get out we will look awful. Dad's legacy will be tarnished, and the members will ultimately vanish. Without members, dad's church will crumble to the ground."

"It's not just his church; I played a major part in building it also."

"Then I suggest you act like it and think of something else."

"Like what? I don't have any other options Maya. We need to act quickly. Your brother is in the beginning stages of his relationship. He's getting to know her more and more each day."

"I think I have an idea. It won't hurt to try it."

"What kind of idea?"

"Remember Vanessa Spellman?"

"Who?"

"Vanessa Spellman, Michael's wife's sister."

"Yes I remember, the real pretty girl with the high-pitched voice."

"Unfortunately, that's the drawback about her. Her voice is kind of annoying."

"Kind of, that girl's voice is a headache waiting to happen. When she starts talking, people start moving away from her searching for Tylenol."

"Mom, but she's beautiful. I caught Jeffrey checking her out one time. I teased him about it, but he shrugged it off and said she wasn't his type."

"What about Ms. Spellman? Has she ever noticed Jeffrey?"

"She has. She asked Michael did Jeffrey have a girlfriend. Michael told her he wasn't into black girls and not to waste her time pursuing Jeffrey."

"So you feel there's a vibe between the two?"

"I honestly do. I'm positive there is. And, she's high yellow; her skin is close to white. And I also know that Vanessa would love the challenge."

"If she can keep her voice down she may have a chance of pulling him in. Is she seeing someone right now?"

"Not that I know of, nevertheless I will look into it."

"How much do you really know about her?"

"I know she's very smart, an attribute that Jeffrey will be attracted to. She was her class valedictorian in high school and graduated with high honors. Vanessa later on attended UNLV and graduated with a bachelor's degree in social work. She works in the DCF office downtown. She's a people person, another plus for us."

"That sounds perfect. How will we get the two of them alone without Jodie being around?"

"It will take some planning out, but I think we can pull it off."

"And you're sure Vanessa will agree?

"If she's not seeing anyone, why wouldn't she? Jeffrey has plenty of money, he's handsome, intelligent, and he knows how to treat a woman." *Unlike Julius.*

"Maya, we need to get this ball rolling. Putting them in the same room together without any distractions may improve our chances."

"I'm on it." I say bye to my mother ending our conversation. It went swell. As a team we can get Jodie out of the picture. Julius steps through the door as I end the call.

"Honey, how was work today?"

"The same as usual, very frustrating; I really hate my job."

"At least you have a job. Do you know how high the unemployment rate is?"

"Like six percent?"

"That's for most whites. For us, it's closer to eleven percent. Just be thankful that you have a job. There aren't too many jobs paying close to thirty dollars an hour without a college education. You're very fortunate."

"I know the pay is good, but I'm bored to death from doing this repetitive labor and putting up with trifling ass passengers."

"What passenger pissed you off today?" *Why did I open my mouth to complain? It doesn't really matter though; she won't know who I'm talking about anyway.*

"Some white lady, wearing a tight ass read mini skirt and a white blouse two sizes too small on Crenshaw Avenue."

"She stood on Crenshaw Avenue wearing that?"

"I lie to you not. What a spectacle. Everyone on the bus stood up to get a peek at her."

"She was looking for trouble then? Did Benny see her?"

"Yeah, he couldn't close his mouth." I laugh.

"Did she talk to anyone on the bus?"

"She introduced herself to Benny. She shook his hand."

"Ooh, I know that made his day."

"It most definitely did. He couldn't stop grinning."

"Good for Benny, he needs a woman in his life."

"She looked to trashy to be with Benny. I think he needs a wholesome woman, not someone who runs the streets and sleeps around."

"How do you know she sleeps around?"

"Just by the way she looks, I can tell."

"I see, so you're an expert on women now?" *He was probably checking her out himself.*

"I never said I was an expert. It's the way she was carrying herself."

"Did you know Benny is getting baptized this Sunday?"

"Yeah, he told me."

"Remember when he joined the church?"

"How could I ever forget it? He was stumbling over every word your father asked him to repeat. Benny was a nervous wreck. So, this Sunday is his big day to have his sins washed away. He's giving himself to God."

"I'm very proud of him. He's made a decision to walk in the light and place his sins behind him."

"Benny looks sinless to me. If he is sinning it's definitely not fornication. I don't think he's ever been with a woman."

"Well, maybe he has one now. The lady in red may be the one he was waiting for."

"You never know, she may be."

"What if Benny invites her to the baptism?"

"Maya, you're moving way too fast. He only shook her hand, it doesn't imply there together."

"I know. I just want Benny to be happy. He's a nice man. He will probably tell me anyway. You know how hard it is for him to keep anything. He loves to talk."

"Amen to that, but if he doesn't offer to tell you please don't ask him about it."

"Why not?"

"I don't want him to think I tell you everything he shares with me." *I'm sure he can share a lot of things about you to me.*

"Oh, this is a man's thing? I get it."

"Something like that."

"Ok, I won't ask if he doesn't volunteer to tell."

"Who were you talking to on the phone when I came through the door?"

"My mother."

"What did she want?"

"Why do you think she wanted something?"

"She never really calls you unless she needs something."

"She didn't want anything. She was just venting over Jeffrey's proposal to Jodie." *I know you're upset too. I'm no fool. I will find out the truth eventually. Trust me.*

"You and your mother might as well leave it alone. There's nothing you can do to change it." *My mother seems to think so. I just hope she doesn't go too far.*

CHAPTER 8

JEFFREY

The nerve of my mother failing to acknowledge Jodie is disheartening to me. Jodie deserves to be accepted into this family like the others. The color of her skin shouldn't be a major concern. My mother opened her arms of welcome when my brothers made their announcements to get married. She went the extra mile catering to their fiancés needs. What does she expect from me? It was her idea to enroll me in all white schools. I became attracted to white girls. I bonded easily with Caucasians and never saw them as a threat. Not once, have I ever had any problems with them and they've never had any problems with me. Most of my complications growing up came from the people in my own neighborhood. They considered me different than most of the kids in the community. Cornball, sellout, and geek, are names they called me which stuck with me throughout high school. I didn't let it hurt me because I knew I was smarter than they were. I had an advantage. My love for learning, lead me down a path my antagonists could not travel. I was ranked number one academically in my high school class. When my peers talked about me, it made me work that much harder to distance myself from them financially. I am now the CEO of a software company in Baltimore Maryland. My mother put me in the right position to start my journey towards success. Now, she wants me to detach myself from the same people that helped me become successful. A white woman isn't good enough for her, but she's good enough for me.

"Jodie, I told you so. My mother is a rare breed. I can't believe her."

"She will not give us our blessing. The way your mother looked at me; I don't ever want to be around her again."

"She's my mother Jodie."

"I know, but she hates me, and I've done nothing to her? She's your mother, and I respect that. But, to be in the same room with her is out of the question." *I can't blame Jodie. If I was in her shoes I would feel exactly the same.*

"Maybe she will change her mind after some time passes by. You know, time mends all things," Jodie gives me a sarcastic look.

"Whatever crystal ball you're looking through you need to look again, because it's not happening. Your mother meant every word she said. She doesn't feel I'm good enough for you. I'm not dark enough."

"Those weren't exactly her words of choice."

"You need to read between the lines, because she doesn't like me."

"I don't care Jodie what she likes or doesn't like. I'm marrying you regardless of what she thinks."

"You will not feel right without your mother's blessing."

"Look on the bright side of things, your parents will be there instead."

"Yes they will, and you will meet them soon enough. I'm positive you'll like them. They're great people. They adopted me at five months."

"Have you ever met your biological parents?"

"No, not ever; I feel there's no need to. They gave me up for a reason. At least they let me live."

"How was it growing up with other adoptive children in the same household?"

"The same as growing up with biological siblings, we didn't see any differences. Our love for one another united us. To this very day we stay in touch."

"How come I haven't met them yet?"

"I've just never got around to introducing you."

"I think we should make the trip. Have you told them about our engagement?"

"Not yet, but I will."

"What if we travel there and surprise them with the news?" I'm sure they would be ecstatic, don't you think?"

"Maybe, you never know?" Derrick and Avery will probably be in shock."

"Why is that?"

"I rather not say. I don't want you to be offended," she looks out the passenger window.

"Sugarplum, whatever you did in your past is in the past. As of now, our relationship is in the present and hopefully continues well into the future and beyond."

"Derrick and Avery were friends with the some of the guys I used to date. I sort of hurt them in some form or fashion by playing with their emotions. I liked to party and being tied down just wasn't my style back then." *Guys?*

"How many guys are we talking about?" She keeps her gaze out the window.

"Not that many. I was young then. I didn't know what I wanted, but now I do," she leans over kissing me gently on my cheek. I don't feel the kiss. I'm too withdrawn from the thought of her being with other guys.

"You still haven't told me how many?" Honey, you can't be serious? I know you're not upset over this? Like you said, the past stays in the past. It has nothing to do with you." *She still won't tell me and I believe I have a right to know.*

"I believe it does. What if you still have feelings for one of these guys? What if they're crazy about you like the stalker guy we took care of? This will impact me as well. I don't like the idea of having to look over my shoulders every time I go somewhere with my fiancée. I want to feel safe when I'm out with you."

"You're feeding into this too much. It's nothing. I don't want anyone but you, and I don't have any stalkers." *There's probably a lot more she isn't sharing with me. I want to be able to trust her. I need her to tell me everything. I've told her everything. If we're going to be together there shouldn't be any secrets kept. Like the manner in which*

Julius watched her. His eyes expressed everything. His stare wasn't one of curiosity. His gaze involved desire, and I'm confident she felt it. I'm no fool.

CHAPTER 9

JULIUS

Why did Jodie board the bus? Our secret was sealed. No one knew about us, not until she opened her mouth up in front of nosy Benny. He listened to the entire conversation. She even had the audacity to flirt with him right behind me. The love and hate I have for Jodie is equal in comparison. As mad as I am from what she's done to me I honestly can't stop longing for her. I go to bed at night fantasizing about the times we made love to each other. Jodie is a firestorm underneath the sheets, and it takes a skilled lover to give her what she needs. I doubt if Jeffrey can even come close to matching her insatiable appetite. If he's incapable she will not stick around. Today is Benny's baptism, and Maya and I are a few minutes away from the church. I'm happy for him. At least he's making an effort to get closer to God. I've been saved, baptized, prayed over, and whatever else you want to call it.

I enjoy going to service, but my recent sins of the flesh have kept me away. It's hard for me to be in God's house knowing I'm not living up to his standards. Maya gets on me a lot about skipping service. I think she gets more upset of the embarrassment it causes her when her family doesn't see me there, especially with her father being the pastor. He's a firm believer on couples being unified with God. Her family spends more time in that building than anywhere else. With the recent discovery of Jodie and Jeffrey being an item I feel less guilty from what I've done. I'm ready to make a change and ask God for his forgiveness. I love Maya and I want God's blessing in our marriage. Her father allows everyone to come as they are inside of the sanctuary. There's no particular dress code as long as your clothes are presentable. It's one of the reasons why I'm comfortable at this church. I can be myself not pretending to be someone I'm not.

"Julius, I can't believe you're attending Benny's baptism. What happened to working on Sunday's for overtime?"

"I declined it even though it was offered to me. I have to be here for Benny. I told my job the overtime is hurting my church time. And from here on out, Sunday's are off limits. My relationship with God and family is more important than a few more dollars in my paycheck," Maya looks befuddled.

"Well, well, well, what has gotten into you? I've been trying to convince you for months and you never wanted to hear me out. Now that Benny is getting baptized you change in an instant?" She appears offended.

"Benny isn't more important than you Maya. I've been putting things into focus lately. Honey, life is too short to waste it on trivial things. I need to get my life in order with God and especially with you."

"Whatever's gotten into you I'm going to leave it alone? I'm just happy you're back," she kisses my cheek.

"I'm happy too." *For how long, I can't say*. We get out of my silver Nissan Maxima and make our way inside.

"Do you think Benny invited his lady friend from the bus? She giggles.

"Maya, she didn't talk to him long enough to be his friend. She only shook his hand."

Inside of the church it's a full house considering it's the forth Sunday and not the first. I didn't expect to see this many people attending. Practically every seat is filled to capacity. The choir is entering the pulpit, and Maya's father is positioned behind the choir dressed in a white robe standing inside the baptism pool along with his wife. *I scan the congregation rest assured that Jodie will not be here. How can she? She's engaged to Jeffrey. She made the news public. It would raise a lot of questions if she showed up here without him. Then again, I wouldn't put it past her. A thought occurred to me. What if she's seeing Benny on the side? No, no, no, I'm being paranoid. Maya has me thinking the wrong things. Jodie isn't that crazy.*

"Julius, there's Benny. He's ready to take his dip in the pool of resurrection. I'm so happy for him. He's making his first step to salvation."

"He sure is."

"Are you alright? You look like you're somewhere else all of a sudden?"

"Yes I'm fine, and I feel great. I'm showing my support for Benny," Maya quickly turns around.

"What's she doing here?"

"Who?"

"Jodie is sitting five rows back, and I don't want you staring at her either."

"Are you sure it's her?" She sucks her teeth.

"Do you think I'm a fool? I know what white trash looks like, and Jeffrey isn't with her. Why is she here today? She's never attended service in this building before." *My temperature rises in my body. How can she be here? She's doing this spitefully. I want to turn around and look at her, but Maya is smothering me. If I turn around it will start a fight. This is Benny's moment. I will not destroy it. For Jodie to be here means she's been staying in contact with Benny. It's the only plausible reason she could know his baptism is today. I apparently underestimated her. She has taken this to a whole another level.*

"I don't know why she's here either, but don't let her rain on your parade. Remember why we're here. You need to stay composed and keep your focus on Benny," she frowns at me.

"Don't tell me to stay composed. You just keep your eyes where they belong. If I see you looking at her I swear I will make a scene in here today," She whispers.

"Maya, you're out of your mind. Our wedding is almost here, and your brother is engaged to her. I'm getting married to you. Why do you continue to berate me over Jodie?"

"Don't play stupid Julius. You know exactly why I'm this way. You've made me this way. I'm a nervous wreck because of you," I hold onto her hand. She tries to pull it back, but I won't let her.

"Maya were in God's house among God's people. Let's enjoy the baptism together and listen to the service in peace. People are beginning to stare. Let's not make a scene. If you're not happy at the moment at least pretend to be for now," she looks around at the congregants staring in our direction and decides to take my advice.

"I will behave. But mark my words, you better behave too," I nod agreeing with her. Her father begins the baptism.

"Today church family I'm pleased to introduce Mr. Benjamin Harold. Mr. Harold works as a Janitor in the public school system and has been cleaning and tidying up rooms for years. He says now is the time for his soul to be cleansed in the baptism pool. He's looking forward to making God a part of his life. Mr. Benjamin would also like to volunteer his time serving the church," the congregation says amen. "Today you are being baptized in the name of the father, the son, and the holy spirit," Maya's father uses his fingers to squeeze Benny's nose. He then grabs Benny by the head and proceeds to dip him in the water. Together, her parents pull Benny out of the water following applauds. After the baptism is completed and they change out of there wet clothing, the choir sings a selection before Maya's father begins his sermon. Benny takes a seat next to us in the pew.

"Congratulations Benny. We're very proud of what you accomplished today," Maya whispers and reaches over me shaking his hand. I extend out my hand as well giving him a firm congratulatory shake.

"I appreciate the support. I was really nervous up there, but your father made me feel comfortable," he utters in a low tone.

"Benny, you looked fine to me. If you were nervous I don't think anyone could tell," Maya acknowledges.

"Julius I can't believe you made it. I didn't think you were coming. When I saw you sitting out here it made me feel pretty good. You know, you and Maya are probably the only real friends that I have. I appreciate everything you guys do for me. I envy the relationship you two have. Julius you are certainly blessed to have a woman like Maya." *What is he insinuating. He's starting already. Don't go soft on me Benny, not now.*

"Benny, that's what friends are for, to support one another. And I agree with you, I am definitely blessed to have Maya."

"He's right Benny, we got your back. And as far as relationships go our relationship isn't perfect. It takes work, but I'm glad you notice."

"Thanks Maya, and thanks Julius."

"Did you invite any of your coworkers to your baptism?"

"I didn't tell anyone at work because most of them don't believe in God anyway. I did tell someone about it, but I assumed they wouldn't show up either."

"Was it a male or a female?" Maya eagerly asks. I quickly cut her off.

"Maya, we're in church. We need to be respectful of that. We can ask Benny more questions when the service is over."

"My father isn't preaching yet, and the choir is singing a selection. And I've heard that same song like a hundred times over."

"Maybe Benny would like to hear them sing? I don't think he's heard it before."

"Benny, have you heard this song before?"

"To be honest Maya, I have. "I Smile", is one of my favorites. The choir doesn't give it justice though, like Kirk Franklin does when his group performs it. I love every song Kirk Franklin has produced. Maya, to answer your question, it's a woman. She was here in the beginning, but it looks like she left. I guess she couldn't stay for the entire baptism." *This conniving idiot is actually talking to Jodie. She has reeled another one in. Are we all suckers for her?*

"Is this something serious Benny?"

"I can't tell. We really don't know much about each other yet." *He has got to be kidding me. If he's seeing Jodie this is becoming stranger by the day. I know he will tell Maya about us, and eventually everyone will find out including Jeffrey. Jodie's engaged to Jeffrey. She's been sleeping with me, and now she's talking to Benny? Could Jodie be this whorish to implicate herself? I don't think so. She is much more sophisticated than that. Benny has to be referring to someone else, and I need to find out whom. I turn my head around while Maya and Benny are talking to see if she's still here. I don't see her. It's definitely her.*

"Did you find what you're looking for?" Maya questions me.

"I'm not looking for anything."

"Then why did you turn your head around Julius? Is it something back there you want?" *She stands up raising her voice which draws attention from the congregation. Our argument is on full display. The choir members are straining to look while carrying their notes. Her father glares in our direction.*

"Don't make a scene in here Maya. You need to go ahead with that. You're being paranoid."

"I'm being paranoid? Your eyes can't stay off of Jodie, and I'm being paranoid? And another thing, I don't care what people think. This is my relationship. Let them look. I really don't care!"

"Julius," Benny interrupts. "I'm sorry but she deserves to know the truth. She's your fiancée, and you haven't been honest with her. Maya, that woman you're talking about rode his bus a few days ago and said some things that..." *Before I allow him to implicate me any further I level him right there in the pew.*

CHAPTER 9

JODIE

J's mother is parading around as an assistant pastor. She's nothing but a two-faced lying bitch. She pretended she didn't know who I was. Maya and I have been friends since college. She's seen me before. I've had dinner at her home. To belittle me in front of J was the wrong thing to do. I see where Maya gets her evil ways from. J is scared of his mother. I will not let her intimidate me. If J wants me to be around his mother it will never happen, and the nerve of Maya to tell her of our engagement before J could announce it is distasteful. I love Jeffrey, but his mother and sister are outright impossible to deal with. If they continue to treat me like an enemy I may just have to move on. I think their jealous of me. I usually get this reaction from black women when I'm dating a black man. What really set Maya off is when Julius had something to say to me. Maya went crazy. Whatever it was it must have been very important, because Julius doesn't say much to me around Maya. He's careful not to trigger a negative reaction out of her. He gives me his undivided attention when I'm talking to Maya, but he keeps his distance. Maya is lucky to have him. She had better take good care of him before he permanently falls into the right hands. He's undeniably a good looking man and would make any women happy. On the flip side of things I think Jeffrey is right. A little getaway to visit my family is probably essential considering the situation. There's just too much tension in the air. Plus, I miss my family a great deal. I haven't seen them in over a year. I feel guilty for not visiting them as often as I should. My mother and father will be happy to see me. I think Jeffrey and I should leave right away an escape the madness.

Benny was partly in shock when Jodie slipped her number to him the day she boarded the bus. He never thought in his wildest dreams a woman of her extent would be interested in someone as plain and simple as him. His looks are third-rate compared to Julius's. Benny dislikes the noticeable bulge around his midsection and is wary of his shortened height as a man. He realizes he isn't ugly, but he senses his face lacks the quality most women find attractive. His eyes are tiny. His face is pudgy, and his thick rimmed glasses give him a dorky unappealing appearance. When he exited the bus that evening he rushed home paying close attention to the time as it seemed to move slower than ever before. The piece of paper she slipped into his palm displayed her number with instructions to call her at 8pm. As the time inched by several thoughts entered his mind. Benny is love struck on how beautiful Jodie appears to be. Her face looks like a goddess, and her smile has set his heart aflame. When she spoke to him her voice became a soothing song to his ears and everything about her radiated goodness. He would never leave a woman like Jodie. She is one of a kind. When 8 pm finally arrived he nervously tapped in the numbers on his cell phone. She answered on the first ring surprising him.

Benny talked to Jodie for hours. She made him feel at ease. It felt like he'd met her before. The two of them suddenly clicked as their conversation lengthened. She explained how Julius came onto her and forced her into a situation she regrets to this very day. Jodie told Benny she wants to set things straight and give Maya the heads up on her cheating fiancée. Benny knew Julius for some years and had just met Maya recently. Jodie explained her indiscretions with Julius and even wept on the phone of how sorry she was for letting him deceive her. When benny heard her cry he cringed inside. The sound of this beautiful creature in pain made him feel obligated to help her. He did exactly what Jodie asked him to do. He attempted to inform Maya of how Julius was misleading her, but his attempt fell short when Julius knocked him out cold inside the sanctuary.

Benny doesn't remember much after that. When he recovered the church was empty, and Maya and her father were the only ones remaining standing over him. Maya expressed to him she knew something was going on between Julius and Jodie, and she vowed to make them both pay for what was done to her and her brother. Maya informed Benny concerning Jodie's engagement to her brother which took him for a loop. Thereafter, Maya sobbed overwhelmingly as she felt her world collapsing. Benny attempted his best pitch to convince her Jodie was forced into doing something she didn't want to do; nonetheless Maya wouldn't have any of it. She demanded there was no excuse for Jodie's betrayal.

Jodie never said anything to him about being engaged. Benny's heart pours out for both Maya and Jodie. He refuses to accept Jodie's engagement to Maya's brother. How can she possibly be with him when the two of them bonded immediately? When Benny makes it back home he repeatedly tries calling Jodie to give her the news. His calls go unanswered. He leaves at least three messages informing her of what took place inside the church. Benny desperately wants to hear her voice. His misses her considerably and can't wait to see her again. She belongs to him, and he promises to keep her. No man or women will stand in his way.

CHAPTER 10

MAYA

The urgent expedition to my parent's home affords me the opportunity to reminisce. I confided in my mother when things were beyond my control as a teen. My mother usually has sound advice to help lift my spirits when things are carrying me over the edge. I hope she can help ease the terrible feeling inside my soul. Julius deceived me, and Jodie helped facilitate it. As far as I'm concerned they're both guilty as charged. I traverse through the traffic on Phelps Avenue making a right turn onto Bishop Street. The area embodies vivid recollections when my brothers and I rode our bikes along the landscape. Bishop Street made us feel safe. The cordial neighbors treated every child on the street as one of their own. Unsafe conditions were unapparent. Everyone knew each other and there was no treachery. Unlike the secure environment I lived in as a child, my current surroundings are completely exposed. The presence of guardians and neighbors to watch over me has disappeared. Evil has found a way in. I run up my parent's stairs and hurriedly turn the key walking inside. My mother sits at the kitchen table.

"I've been calling Jeffrey for over an hour. He won't answer his phone. Where the heck is he? Have you heard from him today?"

"Relax Maya. He's probably busy. He never goes the entire day without calling me."

"Mom, how can you tell me to relax after what Julius has done to me?" My mother takes a sip of her decaffeinated black coffee. She lingers on the taste before answering me."

"It's nothing like a strong cup of coffee in the morning to start your day. I love the smell of it. It puts me in a great mood. Would you like to try a cup?" *I shake my head declining her offer.* "Maya, God doesn't give us more than we can handle in life. I know this treason is very upsetting to you. The man of your dreams has betrayed you along with your friend. It is only a test Maya. Our faith is tested through the fire." *Now is not the time for scripture. I'm dying inside. Why is this happening to me? I've never done Julius wrong. I've been faithfully committed to him.*

"Mom, I know the word. You and dad both have been preaching to us since we were children."

"But you failed to listen, Maya. I strictly warned you against having sex until you were married. When you give a man the milk before buying the cow, what do you expect? You made it easy for him. You gave him everything and he took advantage of you. As women, we have to be careful with our choices. We have to treat our bodies as a temple and a place of adoration, not just stimulation. You wait for a man to love and respect you and show you his true nature. If it isn't evident then you move on."

"Mom, this is the twentieth century. Most men will not wait to have sex. I've tried. And it's nearly impossible to find one that will wait. In the beginning I thought Julius was that person. We waited for about six months before he started pressuring me about satisfying his needs. I love him so of course I gave in."

"Baby, you have to understand something. When the right Christian man enters your life he will wait for sex no matter what. Unfortunately lust is upon all of us because our flesh is weak. To counteract this weakness, we have to surround ourselves with people that have the same things in common as we do. If they're not in our circle we don't invite them into our circle."

"He told me he was a man of faith, and I believed him. He was very sincere at the start of our relationship. Everything about him was so perfect. I'm a fool for believing in him," my mother slams her orange coffee mug against the kitchen table.

"There's neither perfect man nor woman! He deceived you because you put your guard down. Instead of putting God first you worshipped Julius instead. Maya, we all fall short of God's grace. But remember,

God forgives the just and the unjust alike. Place the situation into God's hands and allow him to handle it. Do not seek revenge."

"Mom, all I feel is rage. I want to make them pay for what they've done to me. And you're telling me not to do anything? I can't do that mom. They deserve the worst possible scenario."

"God is not hate Maya. He's unconditional love. If you want God's blessings I suggest you refrain from retaliation. Pray on it, and ask God for his guidance. He will hear you but not with hatred in your heart."

I respect both my parents, but sometimes they're out of touch with reality. Does my mother realize I was getting married in less than a week? I invited so many friends and family to attend. We spent thousands of dollars to make this the best wedding possible. I sacrificed vacations and unnecessary spending to have the funds to put this wedding together. I will be the laughing stock of Baltimore. I believed in Julius and even accepted him with his troubling past in question. To this day I don't know why I honestly believed in him. I considered he was different than most of the men I dated in the past. He did a lot for me and made the disturbing things in my life easier to handle. The day he walked into bible study I firmly presumed he was heaven sent. Before he crossed my path I struggled to find someone suitable for me. I went on a number of dates which turned into nothing but sheer disasters. We had nothing in common concerning God. Sex was more important than communicating. Once they learned of my celibacy they didn't stick around much longer after that, but Julius proved to be different. He knew the bible inside and out. We spent hours going over the word, and he enjoyed my company not just my body. His intentions were honest. Sex was never an issue, at least not in the first six months of being together.

I guess after all the kissing and no touching policy we both weakened in our attempt to remain celibate. I gave in just as much as he did. We both wanted each other from the months of buildup. I'm not entirely upset for giving into sex as much as I am for his infidelity.

I'm a child of God, but how do I go on each day carrying this massive pain inside of me? Julius and Jodie will be held responsible for whatever action I take after today. How else can it be explained? I leave my parent's home feeling worse than I felt when I arrived. How can I pray at a time like this? I wouldn't know where to start. I thought the lord answered my prayers when he sent Julius to me. I prayed diligently and obeyed his words. Why has he forsaken me? If I ever see Jodie again I'll probably kill that whore with my bare hands. I helped her, and she sleeps with my man. What an unrighteous bitch. She will get hers in the end. Julius's ring tone temporarily disrupts my anger. What the hell does he want? I put in my Bluetooth before I answer his call.

"Hello?"

"Maya, before you say anything to me just hear me out. I still love you more than anything in this world. I want you to be my wife. We can still get married. The thing with Jodie was a mistake. I made a terrible mistake, but I don't love her."

"What kind of fool do you take me for? I gave you my world and you destroyed it for a piece of ass. Was my skin not light enough for you? Were my eyes not green enough? Was my behind not big enough? I forgive you Julius. Judge ye not, or ye shall be judged. I can never ever trust you again. My heart won't allow me. You've cut it into pieces, and it will take a very long time for it to heal."

"Maya, I'm only asking for you to give me some time to work this thing out. I know I can do better if you give me another chance. I'm not suggesting today or tomorrow, or even in a couple of months. But in the near future I want to be in your life again."

"Why do you want to be in my life Julius? You had your chance, and you threw it away. The both of you are made for each other. You don't deserve me, and Jodie doesn't deserve Jeffrey. How many times did you sleep with her Julius? Tell me that!"

"Only a few times Maya, it wasn't much."

"Liar! For you to admit it only a few times means it was more like a dozen times! You're disgusting Julius, just plain disgusting. If I have an STD you'll be sorry. I'm going to the clinic the first thing in the morning. You better pray there's nothing wrong with me. So help me God you better pray."

"Why would there be something wrong with you?"

"Your white princess has been around the block and back. I recommend you get checked out also."

"What are you saying?"

"Back in college she screwed anything with two legs. I suppose you thought your charm and good looks had an effect on her, didn't you? She loves sex; more so than the average women. She was fucking you, not the other way around as it might have seemed. And she probably shook your little world to the point of wanting to leave me at the altar alone. Let me tell you something, you can have her. I don't want you, and when Jeffrey finds out the truth he will not want her either. You can fuck each other as much as you want then. Goodbye."

The nerve of Julius to feed me that lame crap to me over the phone, it will be a cold day in hell before I allow him back into my life again. Fool me once, shame on you. Fool me twice, shame on me.

CHAPTER 11

I've never parted on a vacation without planning it first. I believe in being prepared for the unexpected. Jodie insisted that we leave right away. She desperately needs to clear her head concerning the attacks on her character from my mother and sister. To be honest, I can't fault her for wanting to flee. The attacks are undeserving. She's done nothing to either of them to deserve this kind of conduct. Jodie is a good woman. The two of them should be pleased I found someone compatible instead of judging her. Jodie asked me to turn off my cell phone and unplug myself from social media during our trip. I'm having a difficult time honoring her request. My job requires me to be on call twenty-four hours a day. Important transactions are taking place daily in which I need to be aware of. I notified my secretary to take down all of my messages and if it's something extremely important to call Evan McDaniel my assistant. I brought my phone just in case of an emergency, but Jodie made me remove the battery. Both of our batteries remain in her handbag. I'm so accustomed to checking my emails, Facebook, and text messages, that I feel naked without my phone. I guess I'm sort of addicted to social media like everyone else on the planet.

"Do you miss your phone honey?"

"Why, is it that obvious?"

"You look like you've lost your best friend. It's only for a few days. You can survive without it. And besides, it will give us an opportunity to open up to one another. A few days off the grid will enhance our relationship for the better. "

"I know as long as I have you next to me it doesn't matter, everything will be alright," she blushes.

"That's so sweet. When you say things like that to me I really believe you because it's prewired in your DNA. There isn't a bad bone in your body."

"That isn't entirely true. I'm nowhere near perfect. I make mistakes like the next man, but my intentions are good."

"I know you aim to please by what you show me, and it's definitely pleasing to me."

"Jodie, I'll do anything for you, there's no limitation. I truly love you that much. The only thing I ask of you is to be upfront with me. If I'm giving you my all and all I expect the same from you. We're adults. Tricks are for kids."

"I don't have any tricks up my sleeves, only treats, and the kind of treats that keep you coming back for more."

"Is it asking too much if I can have a treat right now?"

"That type of treat will be issued out when we get to the hotel room. I don't think there's enough space inside my car to hand out a treat right now.

"I'm looking forward to it."

"So am I."

Jodie and I check in at a local Holiday Inn. We decide to rest up a bit before visiting her relatives, but instead of sleeping we devour each other for a few hours. Jodie is immediate satisfaction for me. After our brief intermission we shower then hit the road to our destination. Its rush hour and Jodie navigates through the city without a problem. Her parents live in a huge off white Victorian style home two hours away from Baltimore. The median price of each home in the neighborhood is five hundred thousand and up. Jodie looks nervous getting out of the car. Her parents are unaware of our arrival. Jodie insisted on surprising them. Her last visit was more than a year ago. When Jodie presses the doorbell it chimes a classical Beethoven theme for ten seconds. When it ends, a gray haired brown skinned man with large brown eyes and a gray goatee opens the door to greet us.

"Jodie, what a surprise, you know your mother and I was just talking about you?"

"I hope all good things dad," he smiles revealing his overbite.

"Edna and I were wondering when you would come see us again. I can't believe you're here. Edna, there's someone here to see you!" He calls out to his wife before draping his arms around Jodie. Edna grimaces approaching the doorway prudently as her walker patters against the hardwood floor.

"Mom, why do you have a walker? And what happened to you?"

"If you would stay in contact and visit more often you would know what happened to me. I had knee replacement surgery on both knees. It takes six to nine months of recuperation time. I'm doing just fine though, you don't have to worry," Jodie walks over to her and gives her a kiss and a gentle hug. Her mother's short hair is completely white and her tan unblemished round face makes her look younger than her dad.

"I apologize for not staying in touch like I should. There's no excuse. I have to do better. I promise from here on out you will hear from me more often."

"Who is this handsome young man you have standing next to you?" Her mother smiles at me.

"Mom and dad this is Jeffrey, my fiancé. We're getting married next year," her parents look at one another in bafflement.

"How long have you been engaged?" Her father asks.

"A little less than a year, but we love each other so much," her mother angles her head to the side.

"Why haven't you shared this information with us sooner?" Jodie's face is flushed.

"I don't know mom. I just needed to be sure before I told anyone. And now, I'm confident," her parents greet me kindly by shaking my hand.

"That's exciting news. We're happy for the both of you. The two of you come inside and sit down so we can catch up and learn more about this handsome man of yours." Her parent's own a collection of African antiques. There are African masks and an assortment of paintings casing the walls along with miniature ethnic statues in every corner of the living room. The expansive room has plants inside large colorful vases, luxurious furniture, and pictures of children inside a collage above a massive solid oak bookcase.

"Jeffrey, where are you from and exactly what do you do for a living?" Her father asks.

"I'm from Baltimore Maryland, born and raised there. I am the CEO of Balkan Industries. It's a software company. I play the role of chief strategist, product marketer, lead sales person, as well as lead product developer."

"That's wonderful. I bet you keep the ship sailing smoothly."

"In today's competitive market it's a challenge with new technology being produced every day, but I enjoy the work enormously."

"What made you decide to propose to my daughter?" Her mother asks.

"Mom, you just cut straight to the point, there's no beating around the bush with you. I think you're putting him on the spot."

"Jodie, I'm not putting him on the spot. He's obviously in love with you. That I can tell. It's evident in his eyes. I just would like to know how this came about."

"It's ok Jodie. It's a good question. I should be able to tell her why I want to marry you. Your daughter is one of a kind. She's so beautiful. I'm not just referring to her outside appearance, but her kindness and loving heart is beautiful as well. We connected with each other as soon as I met her. She's my all and all. She means the world to me. I would do anything for your daughter," her parents both smile.

"Out of all our children Jodie was undeniably the most well-mannered. She never gave us too many problems growing up. We considered Jodie the second mother in the household. Her siblings occasionally went to Jodie instead of us when they needed help with things. Jodie's maturation process developed quicker than her brothers and sister. As her siblings played with toys Jodie was busying herself with grownup things. Would you like to see the pictures of our children in the collage over the bookcase?" Her mother asks.

"Certainly," her mother painstakingly walks over to the collage with me trailing behind her. The four rows of pictures enclosed in a wooden frame have six photos of each sibling in various activities. In every snapshot two siblings are always included together. As I look closer into the pictures of her family I'm taken aback by what I see."

"My children had a wonderful childhood. Samuel and I made sure of that. We took them everywhere and did entirely everything we could do with them before old age set in. I pushed them academically and demanded my children went to college. I am a retired principal and my husband is a retired heart surgeon. Books were our life, and we made certain books became their life. Each of my children has college degrees and respectable occupations."

"I didn't know Jodie was a twin. She never shared that with me."

"Jeffrey, when Samuel and I lost our first set of twins during my pregnancy we were devastated."

"Edna, you don't have to talk about it. It's going to upset you," she ignores her husband.

"The loss of our children was unbearable for us, and to make matters worse my pregnancies after that ended up the same. I couldn't have children for whatever reason. So, I decided to adopt. I wanted nothing but twins to fill the emptiness inside of me from losing my own. I adopted two twin girls, and two twin boys."

"That is awesome! Jodie, why didn't you tell me you were a twin? You never talk about your sister, how come?" Jodie gives her mother a long stare.

"Jodie, if you're going to marry this gentleman I think he needs to know everything about your sister," her father says.

"Where do I start?" Jodie drops her head.

CHAPTER 12

JULIUS

I lost my composure in front of the entire congregation and will undoubtedly never be able to get Maya back. The truth is I don't deserve anyone as respectable as her. I embarrassed Maya with her family in attendance. Benny did what he thought was right. And to some extent, I can't blame him for telling Maya the truth. But then again, it's the way he went about it. He attempted to put me on blast in front of everyone. I had no choice but to level him before he could finish. There will certainly be repercussions for my actions that took place on Sunday morning. After I hit Benny Maya jumped on me swinging wildly. Her brothers were all present and made a dash toward me. I had no choice but to get out of there as fast as I could. Four against one wasn't in my favor. The odds were stacked against me. After the incidence I've been living under the radar. I put in for an early two week vacation to avoid a confrontation with anyone. My friends have been calling me repeatedly. I don't answer their calls. I need time to myself and time to think. When I'm going through difficult stretches in my life I customarily stay away from everybody. It's just the way I am. I'm too afraid to call Maya to get my things. I hope she doesn't destroy everything I own. As of now, I'm staying at a Best Western hotel. I haven't left the hotel room in two days. I've been taking advantage of room service to accommodate my necessities. They bring whatever I ask for. A knock on my room door startles me. I slide off the bed and tiptoe across the burgundy carpeting to look through the peephole. Why won't this woman leave me the fuck alone? And how did she find out where I was? I crack open the door.

"What do you want Jodie?"

"I want you handsome. I can't get you out of my head. I need to have you at once. Please Julius I beg of you. I'm dying inside."

"How did you find me?"

"I have my ways. You can't hide from me. We belong together."

"I'm done with you Jodie. You've turned my life upside down. I'm hiding out in a hotel because of you. I don't even have a place to live."

"I'm assuming you and Maya are a done deal for you to be in this hotel room. If that's true, I will leave Jeffrey and we can be together forever."

"I thought you loved him. How can you turn it off that easily?"

"I went to Jeffrey to get back at you for not leaving Maya. Now that she's history, I will dump Jeffrey. This is the way it should be. We are meant for each other." *No matter what this woman does to me I have a soft spot in my heart for her. In the very beginning it was nothing but pure lust. I had to have her body and her insatiable sex drive. Standing behind this door I realize I've fallen in love with her to the point of doing whatever she says. I open the door completely letting her inside. The second she walks through the door we remove each other's clothing. She is beyond beautiful. Jodie is a true masterpiece and an impeccable Godly creation which can capture the heart of any man alive. The silky streaks of her long blond hair flow effervescently against her shoulders. Her bodily proportions have me intoxicated with desire. I gently pick her up and carry her to the king-sized bed. I lay her down on the bed.*

"Take me Julius and make love to me. Please make love to me."

Benny's humdrum life has changed in a matter of weeks. Most of the teachers know him at the Martin Luther King Middle school but fail to acknowledge him. He passes through the hallway regularly when taking care of his janitorial duties. To others, Benny seems aloof and peculiar. He keeps his distance for a reason. Benny despises administrators. He believes the only difference between him and administration is a piece of a paper with a title written on it. Degrees and certificates do not make them any better than him. With all their so called knowledge they acquired, he assumes they are clueless in general. Their impoliteness and bourgeoisie attitude towards Benny gives him that impression. The students treat him much better, and he usually goes out of his way to make a student smile if he sees one unhappy. There was a time when Benny looked up to teachers, a period when he fell in love with one. Molly Simms is the eighth grade math teacher. Whenever she notices Benny along the corridor as students hurry to their next class she kindly acknowledges him with a warm salutation. Molly's politeness feels genuine. She doesn't let her position affect the outcome of how she treats people. At times she holds brief conversations with Benny that warm his heart. Molly is an attractive woman. Some of her male students have crushes on Molly and will stare at her instead of focusing on their math in front of them.

Just before Valentine's Day arrived on the calendar Benny had planned out his approach. He bought a box of chocolates and a heartfelt hallmark card to express his feelings towards Molly. He comprehends in the back of his mind Molly is waiting for him to make the first move. She speaks to him every morning smiling beautifully revealing her perfect white teeth and dazzling dimples. Her light brown eyes compliment her bronze skin tone. On Valentine's Day morning Benny pretends to sweep near the lockers across from Molly's classroom two minutes before the bell will sound. His plan is to surprise her when she opens the door to dismiss the class and hand the card and box of chocolates to her. When the bell sounds, the door to Molly's classroom opens as her students quickly exit the room. Normally, Molly would open the door and step outside the classroom to greet him. The card and box of chocolates is underneath his janitorial jacket. He walks over and peeks inside her classroom. Molly is sitting at her desk surrounded by a sea of flowers and reading a large red card. Benny is too late. It seems to him someone had made a move on her before he did. He tries to ease back from the doorway and accidentally bumps into another teacher, Keith Herman.

Benny isn't fond of Keith Herman. Keith Herman is an arrogant two-faced back stabbing women chaser. He befriended Benny when he first arrived to the school. Benny thought Keith had it all together. He and Benny talked about sports and current events and seemed to hit it off well as the months went by. Benny learned soon enough about the real Keith Herman. Benny takes his work seriously as a janitor. He prides himself on cleanliness and never leaves a task unfinished. So, when his supervisor complained of Benny's sloppy work and walked him into the bathrooms he was confused to say the least. There was trash everywhere in sight. It looked like someone had trashed the place deliberately. This went on for a few more times until Benny had to find out who was doing this or else be terminated. It was illegal to place hidden cameras inside bathrooms, especially children bathrooms. Benny had no choice. It was either that, or be fired from the job he loves. He picked up a minute recording device and placed it in a spot where no one would be able to detect it. The next morning the bathroom was trashed again, but this time he would find out who was doing it. First, he cleans up the mess before his boss will discover it, and then he carefully removes the recording device inside the boys and girls bathrooms. On his lunchbreak Benny goes inside the supply room and views the recording. The footage reveals two students trashing the bathrooms together. The students are two of the nicest children you want to meet. Benny can't believe it. Thereafter, Benny approaches each student separately and asks them why would they do this to him?

He tells them if they don't give him a full explanation he will let the principal know of their misbehavior. Keith Herman is behind it. Benny finds out the two boys are Keith's nephews. Keith informed them to keep the bathrooms filthy so eventually Benny would be fired. Keith's brother is unemployed and needed to find a good paying job. If Benny were fired, Keith would help his brother get the janitorial opening. Benny is flabbergasted. How can the same man that speaks to him nearly everyday plot something so deceitful against him? He confronts Keith concerning his scheme, but he denies it. He admits the boys aren't related to him. He claims they are lying to protect themselves and they hate him as their teacher. Benny isn't buying it. So, when Benny accidently bumps into Keith on Valentine's Day morning, a bad taste arises in his mouth. Keith apologizes for his collision and gathers himself. Benny looks him up and down in a repugnant kind of way. That's when Molly appears at the door. She doesn't even notice Benny. She walks over to Keith and tells him the card and flowers are beautiful, and she will accept his offer. It's a date. As the weeks and months came and went, Benny realizes he allowed a man to disrupt his future. He promises himself never again will he allow a man to take what is rightfully his.

Jodie belongs to him and no one will stand in his way of that. Julius is the same two-faced backstabbing liar as Keith Herman. He caught Benny off guard when he punched him inside the sanctuary. But this time, it will be his turn to strike without warning. Benny sits inside a rental car parked a few spaces away from Jodie's white Q40 Infinity. The Best Western hotel parking lot is packed. He spots Julius's car and gets out of his rental walking inconspicuously near his car. He quickly flattens all four tires with a pocket knife and spray paints cheater on both sides of the door in red. Benny walks back to the rear of the rental and opens the trunk. He grabs an aluminum bat out of the trunk of the black Nissan Versa rental. He gets back inside the car before anyone notices him. Squeezing the bat tightly he pulls down the visor looking into the mirror at his crooked nose. Julius broke his nose when he punched him, but this time it will be different. He will break something of his in return and keep him away from Jodie. Keith Herman is in a wheelchair for the rest of his life and Benny believes Julius deserves worst. He slides down in the seat and stares out at the hotel entrance.

CHAPTER 13

JODIE

Sharing information with Jeffrey concerning my sister was probably the wrong thing to do. No one in our family acknowledges her, and we pretend she doesn't exist. I haven't seen my sister in several years, and I pray to God it stays that way. Julia lives her life on the opposite end of the spectrum. She lies. She steals. She cheats. She pretends to be this kind person, but deep down in her black heart it can never be possible. Julia will do whatever she has to do to get what she wants. If you stand in her way she will remove you. I was born two minutes before Julia when our biological mom gave birth to us. My adoptive mom told me she found out that I cried when I came out of the womb, and Julia didn't make a sound. She said Julia's eyes were completely open, almost as if she was focusing on everyone inside the room. That particular trait of observing her surroundings is still apparent. Julia studies things, especially people. She would have made a brilliant detective if it wasn't for her evil ways.

Ever since we were children it has always been a competition thing with Julia. When people see twins as identical as we are they assume the two are connected in a sense. Julia and I have always been disconnected. If I had a boyfriend at the time, she had to have him too. If I had a favorite dress I liked to wear, she had to have it too. Whatever I attained in my life she felt the need to accomplish the same thing. At first, I saw it as a playful thing. She wanted to follow in my footsteps. But then, she took it to an entirely different level. I never fully realized how cracked my sister was until she pretended to be me in front of my friends and colleagues. She did it so well that no one knew it was her.

I will never ever forget the week I was sick. It was my summer break from college. I told everyone I had the flu and was bedridden. The bank where I worked knew I wouldn't be in for at least a week. I told my boyfriend at that time not to come near me because of the flu virus, and I also relayed the message to my friends. The entire time I was recovering from the flu Julia was out pretending to be me. During the week of my sickness I wished I had stayed in bed forever, because Julia had turned my world upside down in a matter of days. Threatening calls were coming from the bank where I worked concerning missing funds. My boyfriend called to let me know the sex we had the other night was amazing, and he couldn't wait until I got sick again if that's what it takes.

My coworker Samantha had also left a message cursing me out for sleeping with her boyfriend. I assumed I was dreaming, but this was far from a dream. It was more like a nightmare with the vision of Julia stabbing a knife in me and twisting it slowly to puncture my heart. To this very day the reason for her betrayal is unclear to me. I questioned her over and over to the point of slapping her for doing what she did to me. She wouldn't answer me. She kept a stone face and said nothing even after I slapped her. From that point forward I didn't want to have anything to do with my sister ever again. My family felt the same way. She is a true menace to our family. My mother misses her quite often. I guess we all do in a sense, but we know how dangerous she can be. The last whereabouts of her location is somewhere near Florida. I hope the sunshine state is bringing her happiness. She looks exactly like me.

Jeffrey and I are eating ice cream at a local Friendly's. He's more aware of the stares we receive than usual, as the people around us are acting like jerks. I glare at the couple across from us, particularly the older white male who seems to be in a trance. He turns his head in disgust.

"Hey, are you ok? Don't let them disrupt the goodtime were having," Jeffrey shakes his head.

"I'm alright. It's just, when will people ever change? They can applaud a man for becoming a woman, but can't or won't accept a black man dating a white woman. It's preposterous if you ask me. Some of your people are downright ignant."

"Don't you mean ignorant?"

"No, I said it as exactly as I attended to say it, the Ebonics version," I laugh lightheartedly.

"My parents seemed to like you a lot. I think my mother was flirting with you."

"She looks good for her age. I bet you she can still turn heads."

"My mother was the more outgoing of the two. She had to force my father to go anywhere. He was a regular workaholic. I think he believed in the God complex. When he operated on patients he felt it was his hand saving them instead of God's."

"Are you a true believer?"

"That, I am. I just don't attend service enough, but I do read my bible in private." He is looking at me like he doesn't believe me.

"I've never seen you read it."

"Did you forget the private part?

"I'm a true believer also. Not just because my mother and father run a church together. I know God is real. And if you know God is real, why not forgive your sister then? I give him a shrewd look.

"I have forgiven my sister. I just don't have to be around her. She is not a part of me."

"But, you two are identical. When I looked at the pictures I couldn't tell if it was you or Julia. She is very much a part of you. How bad can she really be?" *Where is he going with this? He doesn't know Julia like I know Julia. If he ever meets her he will change his optimism.*

"I explained how bad she can really be already. Let me ask you something. How well do you really know me?"

"I think I know you pretty well. I've been with you for about a year, and I know most of the things you like. I can tell when something is bothering you. I can also tell when you're happy. I can honestly say I know the person sitting in front of me."

"What if I told you I was Julia? How could you tell the difference?" He ponders for a moment pulling on his neatly trimmed goatee.

"I guess I wouldn't be able to. There's no distinction, not one I can see from the pictures."

"There is a distinction. I will only share it with you if you promise to stop talking about my sister."

"Is it bothering you that much?"

"It really is. I want to enjoy my time away with you. So can you please talk about something else instead?"

"Ok, I will change the subject. Forgive me for being overly talkative. I'm going through social media withdrawal. It's been hours since I checked the web. I'm unplugged, and I feel so lost," he looks confused.

"Honey, it's not that bad. I'm unplugged just like you, but I have an idea. Why don't we plug into each other instead?" He cracks a smile and reaches over the table to kiss me to the dismay of the senior citizen across from us. I put more tongue and cheek action into it just to piss him off. He gets up with his wife and throws his tip against the table and walks out of Friendly's.

"We have another satisfied customer honey."

"I'm glad he enjoyed our service. I hope he recommends others," Jeffrey bursts out laughing and I join in with him. The waitress picks up her tip and wipes down the table. Shortly after, a group of four black females sit inside the booth next to us. Jeffrey's expression turns sour in minutes. He looks extremely uncomfortable. He doesn't even move his neck to look in their direction. I hear them muttering to each other as we finish up our ice cream. I know they're talking about us because of the stares; nevertheless I have to be careful not to draw a reaction from them. If I decide to open up my mouth it just might set it off in this restaurant. If they want to stare at us with disapproval I have no problems with it, as long as they don't touch me. I swing my hair deliberately to give them something more to talk about. Two of them roll their eyes at me.

"Jeffrey, how was your ice cream honey?" Jeffrey keeps his face forward. He softly clears his throat.

"The ice cream was delicious."

"I bet it isn't more delicious than me," I say it loud enough so the four women can hear. They cut their eyes on Jeffrey. He tenses up but comes through.

"The ice cream doesn't stand a chance," I smile at him. The women suck their teeth.

"Do you like my eyes J?"

"I love your eyes.

"Well, the only way to tell the difference between Julia and I is a small blemish surrounding her retina. Julia has a small discoloration inside her eye that you can only see when she cuts her eyes to the right. It's the only way to tell us apart. So, now you know just in case you run into her. But, I think were safe. Now, let's get out of here. We have unfinished business to take care of back at the hotel."

CHAPTER 14

MAYA

The entire day has ended and not a word from Jeffrey. I have a gut wrench feeling Jodie is behind this. She can't hide him forever. My brother will find out the truth eventually. I will make sure of it. There's a saying which states most people convey two faces. The one they want you to see and the one that remains hidden. I thought I knew Jodie pretty well, but I was terribly mistaken. The woman has a serious problem. She's seeing three men at the same time and two of whom don't belong to her. She might as well quit her job and stand on the street corner and become a prostitute. Jodie opens her legs to everyone just like in college. She hasn't changed a bit, and the men haven't changed either. They're still chasing her tail. I turn off my lamp and shut my eyes to get some rest. The next morning I check my phone to see if Jeffrey has called. My call log is empty. I shower, eat breakfast, and make my way to work. Inside my office I stare at the computer screen. I'm still faced with an unbalanced ledger. My numbers are off by thousands of dollars unaccounted for. Where have the funds disappeared to? I have to report it to my superior. I've searched every possible loophole and nothing has turned up. I hate to assume the worst, although I believe someone is embezzling money from the company. I have to find out before they implicate me. I'm the accountant and the first person to be investigated when money is missing. As I continue to rack my brain and find out what is happening there's a solid knock on my door. I politely tell them to come in. When the door opens my boss walks in with two security officers standing behind him, and he doesn't look happy.

"Maya, if you were in financial straits all you had to do was ask me for help. I would have done everything in my power to assist you. You're one of my best employees. Did you think I wouldn't find out thousands of dollars were missing? What sort of fool do you take me for?"

"I didn't take the money. Mr. Pearson, I'm not a criminal. I'm your accountant. I've been working around the clock desperately to find the missing funds. You have to believe me." Mr. Pearson towers over the security guards in my office. Rumor has it he played basketball in his collegiate days. His wiry frame and lanky six feet four stature makes him look even more menacing standing in front of my doorway.

"Maya, even if I wanted to believe you I couldn't. There are just too many discrepancies. You left a trail so wide and long it was impossible for me not to pick up on it. I am amazed at your savviness and the sheer boldness of you believing you would get away with it. I will not press charges on you just yet. I'm giving you a week to return all monies that are missing. If I don't receive the missing funds in the allotted time I will have no choice but to have you arrested. You have brought shame to this company. We trusted and believed in you. I suggest you get your things and leave out of here at once, or I will have you escorted out of the building." *I feel the need to state my case and fight for my job, but from the looks of things arguing my point would be a no win situation. Mr. Pearson's mind is already made up. He has evidence. I've never stolen anything in my entire life. I'm not a thief. This is not right. I want to cry. I want to scream, although I will not give him the satisfaction. If he wants to get rid of me so be it. I'm a very smart woman. I will bounce back from this. I will definitely get a lawyer and sue this company. If he wants to play hardball let the game begin. The thought of being escorted out of the building where everyone can see is not something I'm looking forward to. I grab my belongings. Clear my desk. And leave out of there without a fuss. The tears I valiantly fought back inside my office lastly make their way down my cheeks. Yesterday my fiancé commits infidelity and today my employer fires me. Where do I go from here? How do I put the broken pieces back together? I throw everything in the trunk of my car and hastily jump in the front seat and pull away from my parking space. I slam on breaks as Gertrude steps in front of my car without warning. I let my window down.*

"Gertrude, have you lost your mind? I could have killed you," she runs over to my window with her hand firmly pressed against her chest breathing heavily. Gertrude places her oversized flowered handbag on the ground. Her salt and peppered hair is tied in a bun and her forehead is dampened from perspiration.

"I'm so sorry Ms. M. I just heard what happened to you. I got to the parking garage as quickly as I could. It's just terrible how you were treated," I wipe my eyes trying to conceal my tears. "I feel so bad. Will you be alright Ms. M.? Do you need anything?"

"I just need time to think. I've never been fired from any job. I'm still in a state of shock. The company was so good to me and then out of nowhere they terminate me. It's a lot for me to handle, but I will get through it."

"Did you ever talk to Thomas?" Her gray eyes link with mine.

"I tried calling him, but he won't accept my calls. His secretary told me I need to make an appointment just to talk with him."

"That spells cover up. He's hiding something. He's avoiding you for a reason."

"What reason would that be?" She bends down slightly to go into her bag.

"Here, this is for you," she hands a manila folder to me and then straightens her gray skirt.

"What is this?"

"I think you will find it very interesting, especially where funds are concerned."

"You have found where the missing funds are going?"

"Not exactly Ms. M. but there is a number of accounts which may spark your interest."

"You are definitely working below your pay grade. When this is all said and done. I will help you pass the bar exam. The judicial system is missing out terribly," she forms a light smile.

"That life is behind me Ms. M. I don't ever want to see another bar exam."

"Gertrude, I will look over the details. If I find something noteworthy I will call you right away. I proceed through the parking area."

"Ms. M., please keep in touch," her Jamaican accent resonates in the background as I drive off.

"I promise I will Gertrude," I yell out the window.

Mr. Pearson will prosecute me in a week if I'm unable to discover the source of the missing funds. Instead of driving home to cry alone I detour to my parent's church. I remember as a child the first time I got on my knees to pray. I had lost my dog and was stricken with grieve. Prince, a small Pekinese terrier, had become an important part of my life then. At the age of six I didn't have many friends. I was the only girl in the family. The boys had each other, and at times I felt left out. I refused to play with cars and I detested sports. I wasn't a tomboy. I begged my mother for a dog and she gave in as long as I promised her I would help take care of him. I took him for walks, fed him, and bathed him when it was time for his bath. Prince followed me wherever I went. He was my sidekick and we were inseparable. Then out of nowhere Prince disappeared one morning. I think my dad accidently left the front door open and Prince went outside and never returned. I cried for weeks. My mother offered to get me another dog, but I didn't want another dog. I wanted my sidekick. My father felt awful for not closing the door. He apologized to me and gave me a big hug to console me. He then spoke to me about God. He said if I get on my knees and bow my head and pray with an open heart and mind, that God would hear my prayers and answer them. I prayed to God asking him to bring Prince back to me every day and night for three months. Then, it happened. One morning when I went to open the front door to go to school Prince was sitting there wagging his tail. I was so overjoyed I skipped school that day. My mother said it was okay to miss a day because it was a special occasion. From that moment forward I've been praying to God with an open heart and a sound mind when things are above my control.

When I walk inside the sanctuary I observe the room. This room has been a staple of our family for many years. When my father quit his job some number of years ago as a machinist and told my mother he received a calling from God to minister, she nearly lost her mind. How would they support five children without a steady income? My mother went ballistic. She threatened to leave my dad if he didn't get his act together. He steadfastly believed in God's words. His faith never wavered in the times he struggled to provide for our family. He preached on street corners, inside barbershops, and sometimes inside school auditoriums until he eventually found a building of his own. The abandoned building, once a liquor store had promise to it. He cleaned out his entire savings and was fortunate enough to win the Baltimore lottery for three million dollars. With the help from his family it became a newly designed church. I kneel down gazing at the vast magnificent cross made of timber just above the pulpit. I bow my head stretching out my arms to begin my prayer.

"Lord of lord, and king of kings, please hear my voice. I am just a speck of dust in your presence. I am not worthy of all the things you have given to me already. I am a sinner and sometimes sin takes control of me. Lord, will you forgive me of my sins and any transgressions I have against anyone. Lord, take away the anger and hatred I have for those who have done wrong things to me. I forgive them. I humble myself before you. God, help me to find justice in an unjust world. Lord, I call on you to avenge me. Lord, fill me with knowledge and understanding to recognize evil when it is present. Protect me against the dealings of the devil. Give me power and strength to defend myself. I need your help, and I need it now. My mind is troubled and my burden is heavy. Help me to carry the weight on my shoulders. I pray that you look after Jeffrey and keep him in your care. I ask of these things in Jesus name I pray, amen." I get back to my feet. I wipe my face and head out of the church. I feel so much better. The spirit has lifted me. I feel lighter as I walk to my car. Just as I'm turning out of the driveway

Julius's ring tone chimes loudly. I will not allow the devil to intercept my blessing. When we call on God, the devil answers also. I ignore the call. What does he want, and why should I give him the time or day? He's made his bed, and I'm positive he's laid down in it many times with Jodie.

CHAPTER 15

JEFFREY

It feels wonderful to be plugged back into social media. My phone has been off for two days. No sooner than I turn my phone back on, twenty voice messages instantly pop up from Maya. As Jodie steers through the stream of traffic I listen to each urgent message. All of her messages reiterate the same thing, to call her right away. I quickly dial her number and wait for her to answer.

"Where have you been? She answers on the third ring. I've been trying to reach you for two whole days."

"I skipped town for a while. I took a mini vacation."

"In the middle of the week without telling anyone, and having your phone turned off? What kind of mini vacation is that? You usually keep mom in the loop, but you didn't even bother to call her. This is not like you Jeffrey. Is that woman with you? I know she put you up to this."

"She has a name. I suggest you use it," Maya stays silent for a moment.

"She has a lot of names. Some of which I will not say at this time. I can't believe you Jeffrey. Open your eyes up to the truth. She's deceiving you. Do not trust her," Jodie turns the music down on the radio.

"Is that Maya?" Jodie whispers. I nod acknowledging it is. Jodie expresses her displeasure by hitting the steering wheel.

"What is so important to leave twenty messages on my phone?"

"I will tell you when you get back. I don't want to say it with her riding in the car with you. It's extremely important, for your ears only."

"My ears are her ears, so whatever it is you have to say to me I suggest you say it with Jodie right next to me."

"Why are you being difficult? Just trust me. I'm your sister, remember?"

"If you were a genuine sister you would've accepted my engagement to Jodie already with no questions asked. Not turn your back on me like you've done."

"I've nullified this relationship because I care about what happens to you. You shouldn't be with her. She will destroy you Jeffrey. Get out before it's too late."

"I will not do such a thing. I love her, and if you refuse to accept it then it's your lost, not mine."

"She's been playing you for a fool the entire time. She has slept with Julius behind your back." *Listening to her mention Julius name angers me.*

"I will not listen to your lies so you can persuade me to leave her. Jodie and I are very happy together and we respect each other. The thing you're signifying has no validity. Did you catch the two of them together somehow? Where is your proof?" *Jodie rolls her eyes.*

"I didn't catch them in bed together Jeffrey, but a reliable source told me everything I needed to know."

"How reliable is this source?"

"Extremely reliable, as a matter of fact he saw your so-called fiancé board Julius's bus sometime last week and exchange heated words that meant they were together previously."

"Who is this person?"

"That is for me to know and for you to use your brains and find out. This person has even spoken with your fiancé intimately." *I don't appreciate Maya blowing up my phone and playing games. This person and that person is not enough for me to believe in her lies. She will say and do anything to break us apart.*

"Look Maya, I don't like charades. You have to do better than that to make me believe my fiancé is playing me. I have to go now. I want to enjoy my time with Jodie."

"Jeffrey, you're making a huge mistake. This woman will end up burying you. Ask her about all the men she slept with in college. Jodie shook her ass for everyone on campus. I would love to see the look on her face when you mention it to her. I told her to stay away from my brothers, and I meant it. I didn't want to air her dirty little secrets, but she left me no choice. I have to fight fire with fire."

"What... are you saying?" *I know good and well what she's implying. I just need to hear it again, to be certain my ears aren't failing me.*

"Your fiancé has been around the block and back. She slept with men on campus to get money from them. Some wore protection, some didn't. It depended on how deep their pockets were. She cashed in on her assets. Sooner or later she will take you to the bank as well. It's only a matter of time before she makes a withdrawal." *The lump in my throat makes it problematic for me to respond. I swallow hard while trying to keep my composure. The thought of Jodie in uncompromising positions with different men to make money turns my stomach. It's hard to keep my poker face as Jodie glances at me from time to time."*

"Honey, end the call with her. It's obvious that she has upset you. You're allowing her to get to you. Jeffrey, please end the call." *I open my mouth to respond, but nothing comes out. It feels like my heart is wounded. As I sit here speechless, Jodie grabs the phone out of my hand.*

"Maya, I believe you're done. You've said what you had to say. Jeffrey and I will not listen to it anymore, good bye," I drop my head into my hands. "J, don't let her get to you. I told you in the very beginning she would do this to us. She will not stop until were separated. I warned you over and over, but you insisted Maya would change over time. It surely doesn't look that way to me." *Her words fall on deaf ears. How could she give her body to all of those men on campus? Where's her self-respect? I've kissed and made love to a woman having a collection of lovers. How many college men have entered into my fiancé unprotected? How many had diseases? How many times did she sleep with each guy? Is she a sex addict or just a plain whore? My thoughts are running wild and my head is pounding from the mental anguish. I need some air. I need to breathe.*

"Jodie, can you pull the car over for a minute?" She looks at me with concern.

"J, what is it? Why do you want me to pull the car over on the highway?"

"Just pull the damn car over and stop asking me questions," I yell at her. She pulls over without saying another word.

"I need some air. It's hard to breathe in here," I get out of the car.

"But I have on the ac, and you were fine before the phone call. Jeffrey, please tell me the truth. What did your sister say about me? I know she said something because you're acting strangely." *If I discuss it with her I will probably end up hitchhiking back home. I feel betrayed and helpless. I can't even look her in the eyes. I turn my back to her facing the shrubbery near the passenger door. The cars on I-95 are zipping by on the four lane highway.*

"Is there something you would like to tell me Jodie?" *I pick with the shrubbery never turning around to give her eye contact.*

"How can you ask a question without looking at me J? It must be pretty bad for you not to be able to look at me. Are you feeding into your sister's shit?"

"She said some things I don't want to believe. I have to question you about it. If I don't, it will eat away at me. I pray to God it isn't true. If it is, I don't know if I can go further in this relationship."

"Jeffrey, can you please turn around and face me before you get poison ivy? You're not making any sense right now. What has she said to make you feel like this?" *I drudgingly* turn *around to face her. I know her past is her past and I shouldn't hold it against her. But, how can I not think about the many men that have penetrated her? It pains me to think the love of my live has opened her legs for money. Does she truly love me, or is she after my money also? I'm not rich, but I do make a very comfortable six figure salary. My portfolio is stocked with numerous business investments. My thoughts about Jodie's past are quickly wiped away from the screeching tires of a tractor trailer bearing down on us swerving out of control. The rig is whirling toward us as the truck driver tries to straighten it out. I jump in Jodie's car and tell her to pull off. She starts the car, after which a loud noise from the rear shakes the frame and sends us spiraling several feet into the air. When the car touches the ground we flip over again and again and again. The car is upside down and I'm disoriented. I have glass digging into my face and neck. Blood is everywhere, but there's no sign of Jodie. I try to maneuver myself out of the car, but I don't have enough strength. The scenery on I-95 becomes blurry. Everything begins to fade into the darkness. I hear sirens at a distance and voices of motorists who have left their cars to assist me. I don't hear or see Jodie. Where is Jodie? I have to find Jodie. I try earnestly to free myself, but the darkness consumes me as I drift further away.*

CHAPTER 16

JULIUS

I reneged on my promise. I allowed Jodie to seduce me. I told myself I would never touch her body again. Why do I continually let this woman manipulate me? Is she that alluring to completely cloud my senses and my judgement? I know I shouldn't be with her; nevertheless I just can't seem to get enough of her. We've been going at it for hours. Dusk has appeared outside. Time swiftly ascends when the two of us are together. Jodie gets out of the bed and struts naked along the carpet entering the bathroom. She's a beautiful specimen. As much as I want to discontinue our carnal escapades, my loving core and ferocious lust enslaves me. Will I ever be able to make things work with Maya? I still love Maya. She will make the perfect wife. Maya is a woman I can trust. Could I ever trust a woman like Jodie in a long term relationship? My jealously will drive me over the edge. If I ever see a man near her it will trouble me. Jodie jumps back into the bed kissing me softly on my lips.

"I love when we spend time together Julius. I wish I could stay here with you for the rest of my life. I don't want anyone but you. Do you feel the same for me?"

"I... do Jodie. I just don't feel right for the way I'm disrespecting Maya. I played with her emotions, and she never would've done that to me. Let me ask you a question Jodie. Don't you feel somewhat guilty of how we took advantage of Maya?"

"Not at the very least. You and I deserve to be happy. Just like everyone else in the world. Maya failed to make your heart content. It's the reason why you chose me instead." *Where are her feelings?*

"I can't believe you don't feel anything from betraying your friend?

"She isn't a true friend. If she was, she would've been happy for Jeffrey and me when we informed her about our engagement. Instead, she criticized my character in front of him. What kind of friend does something like that?"

"I guess you make a valid point. I thought Maya would have been thrilled with the idea of you two together. She was more upset than I was."

"Well Julius, you don't have to be upset any longer. I have left Jeffrey to be with you. And Maya is out of the picture I assume, unless you still want to marry her?"

"No."

"No what?"

"No I don't want to marry her." *I'm lying to Jodie. I miss Maya significantly. I didn't want things to turn out like this. I've made a huge mistake, but how can I turn it around? This is the last time I will sleep with her. I swear to it. I can't do this anymore.*

"Then what's with all the guilt? Remember in the beginning of our relationship when you told me Maya had put you through so much to be with her? Her addiction to drugs nearly broke you two apart. You battled for her and accepted her the way she was. You helped her to get clean, because her family refused to have anything to do with her. Haven't you sacrificed plenty? You shouldn't feel guilty. I honestly believe you've done enough for her. Didn't you tell me you thought she was using again? It's time for you to move on to bigger and better things."

"Sometimes Jodie you can be so heartless. I did say those things about Maya. She struggled with her addiction for a long time. I don't know how she will cope with this recent distress in her life. Heroin was her drug of choice. It had become her coping mechanism to withstand her problems. Heroin suppressed her shortcomings and failures until she understood through rehab how to deal with adversity in a more manageable way. She has been drug free for five years. Not a very long time, but she's a fighter. I just don't know how much she will be affected by this." *Jodie's expression and body language remains unchanged. She looks as if she can care less from what I just said. She jumps on top of me. I want to push her off of me, but I don't resist. Her emerald green eyes penetrate into mine as she forces her tongue inside my mouth. I am instantly aroused as my thoughts regarding Maya begin to diminish. Jodie kisses me harder devouring my oxygen. She caresses and teases, forcing me to want her more and more. My body weakens under her spell. I lastly give in. Sleep had fallen upon us after we made love for a second time. I get out of the bed leaving Jodie to dream in comfort. She looks angelic sleeping peacefully. I throw on my shorts and a white beater and peer out of my hotel window. I pull back the tan curtains slightly scanning the parking lot. I can see Jodie's car from my third story window. Her white Infinity stands out amongst the rest of the solid color cars. She's parked two rows behind me. I transfer my attention to my vehicle and can't believe my eyes. Someone has flattened my tires and spray painted my car with red paint. The word cheater in large gravity like letters is emblazoned on each door. How did Maya find out my location? I didn't tell anyone of my whereabouts, not even Jodie. Maybe Jodie was unaware she was being followed. She has brought more trouble than I can tolerate. I jump when Jodie touches me.*

"What's gotten you spooked all of a sudden?"

"Take a look out the window."

"Oh my God, who did that to your car?"

"How do I suppose to know? I've been in here the whole time with you."

"Do you think Maya would do this?"

"Who the hell else? She definitely has a motive."

"Did she know you were staying here?"

"No one knew I was staying here. I made sure of it. And how the hell did you know I was staying here?"

"I sort of tailed you."

"What is this, surveillance? Are you a damn detective?"

"No silly, I'm not a detective. I just needed to know where you were."

"And it seems to me like Maya knew where you were."

"I would've noticed her tailing me. I'm a very observant driver."

"I think you were unobservant today, because look at my car. It's ruined."

"Let me see if I can spot her car in the parking lot."

"Don't you think I've already done that?"

"It doesn't hurt to check again."

"You're opening the curtains too wide. If she's still out there I don't want her to know what floor I'm on."

"Ok Julius, take it easy. Don't go postal on me."

"I'm glad you're finding humor in this. My car is destroyed and you think it's a joke. Every time you show up something bad happens. I can't do this anymore Jodie. You have to leave me alone."

"Relax Julius, I don't see her car. If she did do this to you she left already."

"Who else could have done this to me? She had every reason to do it," she continues to peer out through the curtains.

"I think I see your problem."

"She's out there?"

"No, but someone else is."

"Who?"

"Take a wild guess."

"Benny?"

"Yes."

"What the hell is he doing out there?"

"Following me."

"And why would he be following you?"

"I led him on just a little."

"What kind of woman are you Jodie? Did you spread your legs for him too?"

"Not exactly, I toyed with him to get back at you for treating me so rudely on the city bus."

"Does he have your number?"

"Yes, and I think he knows where I live." *Lord, please help me.*

CHAPTER 17

JODIE

Julia showered. Gathered her belongings, and was nearly thrown out of the hotel room by Julius. Before he slammed the door in her face she managed to blow him a soft kiss. He frowned in return warning her to stay away from him. She threw herself against the door after it shut, lingering there for a moment wanting to feel his heat once more inside of her. Julius made her feel alive. His passionate lovemaking invigorated her spirit. She needs him in the mornings. She needs him in the evenings, and she definitely needs him as of this moment. Benny has become a pest. His interference is not what she expected. She assumed Benny would get the picture when she stopped contacting him. If the damage to Julius's car was done by him, what kind of person does that make Benny? Julia hasn't even kissed him. They talked on the phone for at least a week before she disallowed it from going any further. She walks toward the elevator with laboring steps. Once inside, she presses the button for the lobby. As the elevator descends from the third floor Julia's sweeping thoughts regarding her family intervene. How dare they disown her? It's been several years since she last seen her family and her rage for each one cannot be contained any longer. Her prime target is Jodie; destroyer of her life, her twin, and her nemesis. Jodie is the sole person responsible for her exodus. Jodie took away everything she loved causing her insoluble pain. She has infiltrated Jodie's circle and soon she will feel her fury.

When Julia reaches the lobby she departs out of the building into the darkness through the rear to avoid being spotted by Benny. It's a full moon and the night is serene. She walks around the side of the hotel tiptoeing to stay clear of him. When she reaches the end of the building she stops before taking any further steps. His car is parked two rows behind hers, and he's concentrating on the front door. Julia hadn't realized she flirted with a psychopath. Her life is certainly in peril. If she jumps in her car and takes off he will probably follow her to the ends of the earth. He's nothing but another basket case to her, and she has met her share of them. Julia vacates the security of the building and remains far-off to the right of the parking lot. She inconspicuously approaches the rental he's sitting in from the rear with caution. As soon as she moves in closer to get his attention Julius walks through the front door of the hotel entering the parking lot. Benny jumps out of the rental going after him with an aluminum bat in his hand. Julia yells out to Benny to prevent him from attacking Julius.

"Benny, what are you doing out here?" Startled, he turns around glaring at her.

"I should be asking you that same question. Why haven't you answered my calls?"

"I didn't think I had to answer your calls. You are not my husband, and you're not even my boyfriend. I had a few conversations with you over the phone, that's it. I don't owe you anything." The black aluminum bat is dangling in his right hand. His eyes are simmering with contempt.

"So you think you can just use people, is that it?" He moves forward. Julia takes a step backward.

"I didn't use you Benny. I never told you we were in a relationship. How did I use you?"

"You flirted with me. You made me believe you wanted me just as much as I want you."

"I'm sorry if you took it the wrong way. I was only trying to get back at Julius. I shouldn't have involved you," Benny throws his head back in disgust. He then inhales and exhales deeply while getting a full glimpse of the sparkling moon."

"You know people say crazy things happen when there's a full moon out? And I honestly believe it, especially how things are turning out tonight. Just look at the moon. It's beautiful, it lights up the entire city," Julia ignores him taking another step backward. "Did you hear me? I said look at the damn moon Jodie!" Frightened from his tone of voice, Julia tentatively looks out at the moon.

"It... is beautiful."

"The moon gives life to a darkened metropolitan, the same manner in which you light up my miserable life. You have brought me happiness, and I don't ever want it to end. We will make a great couple. You told me you thought I was handsome. You said you cared for me," Benny's glasses are fogging up from the humidity. He takes them off to wipe the lenses on his shirt and fails to notice Julius creeping up on him in his peripheral vision. Before he can put his glasses back on Julius grabs the bat out of his right hand and pushes him to the ground. His pudgy body rolls over a couple of times as his lenses crack from hitting the ground. He places the glasses back on his face looking up at Julius through fractured lenses.

"Benny, did you do this to my car?" Benny doesn't say a word. Julius jabs the fat end of the baseball bat into Benny's ribs. He yells out grimacing.

"I will ask you one more time. Did you do this to my car? I want an answer." Benny looks over at Julia. He can see two of her through his broken lenses. And he doesn't know which one to focus on; they're both beautiful and distrustful.

"Answer him Benny. Did you do this to his car?"

"If I did do it he deserved it. He punched me out in the church and broke my nose, and he's cheating on Maya. He doesn't belong to you. You belong to me. We have something special," Julius jams the bat into his rib cage a second time. Benny cries out again.

"Benny, you and Jodie are testing my faith. I'm trying to live better and do things differently in my life. Jodie, I don't need your temptation, and Benny, I don't need your animosity towards me. I will forgive the both of you. Benny, I had this coming from hitting you inside the church, so consider us even. I'm sorry for what I've done to you. Now, if you fuck with me anymore I won't be this nice the second time around.

Benny, you two belong with each other, Mr. and Mrs. deranged. Jodie, stay the hell away from me. And I mean every word of it. I'm done. I want my fiancé back. I just hope it's not too late. Benny, get in your car and get the hell out of here before I beat the living daylights out of you. And Jodie, that goes for you too."

After speaking with the doctor inside the hospital I feel numb. Jeffrey and I are lucky to be alive. I suffered only a few scrapes and bruises after being flung across the highway. My seatbelt saved my life. I crawled out of the car to get help, because Jeffrey was too disoriented to move on his own. Compared to my minor scrapes and bruises Jeffrey suffered the worst of the ordeal. The trauma to his head from the tractor trailer's impact caused him to lose his memory. Jeffrey is unable to remember his name and doesn't know who I am. The doctor said it could take months before his memory fully returns. He told me I should notify his immediate family so they can give him the proper care he needs. Jeffrey's in no condition to work or do anything stressful or strenuous. He needs to recuperate in a relaxed environment with indirect cues to bring back his memory. If I notify those two witches that hate me I will probably never hear from Jeffrey again. Once they learn of his memory loss my name will go unmentioned in their scheme to replace me. I definitely can't kidnap him, but I don't want to lose him forever. I'm selfish in a sense, but not that selfish to keep him away from his family. I have to do the right and honest thing, even if it means losing Jeffrey in the process. I just have to believe his memory will return in time so we can be reunited again. If it's meant to be it will happen.

Before making the call to his family I enter the hospital room where they are keeping him. He is drifting in and out of consciousness. They have given him some strong pills for the pain he's feeling. I walk over to the bed. I gently squeeze his hand. He looks at me unfamiliarly. I smile at him. He doesn't smile back. His eyes are searching mine for clarity as my face is unrecognizable to him. He looks lost in his attempt to identify me.

"It's ok Jeffrey. Try not to think so much. Your memory will return in time."

"Is that my name, Jeffrey?"

"Yes."

"And where was I born?" He asks touching his head grimacing.

"You were born in Baltimore Maryland. It's where your family lives."

"Do I have any brothers or sisters?"

"You have four brothers."

"What about sisters?" *She's dead. I didn't mean that.*

"You have one sister."

"When will I see them?" *I hope never, but it's not up to me.*

"They will be here soon to pick you up."

"What is your name?"

"My name is Jodie," he gazes at me.

"You are very beautiful. Are you my wife?" *I was planning to be your wife, but now our plans will change.*

"No, I'm your fiancé," he reveals a slight smile.

"It's a shame I can't remember you," he closes his eyes wandering off to sleep.

CHAPTER 18

I've lost my job along with the man I loved in the same week. How much worse can my life become? Where do I go from here? How do I fix the broken pieces? Sitting here dwelling on my downfall will only take me back to a place I courageously wrestled to escape. I'm a recovering addict, and every day is a challenge for me. I have to remain positive and keep my emotions in check. I walk a different path now, a path filled with rediscovery and opportunity. I've come so far to reconstruct my life. I must fight not to allow my demons to get the best of me. How ironic to think the person that supported me in my struggle with drug addiction is the same person facilitating my return. Julius was my drug dealer at that time. He sold Heroin to me. I did anything and everything to get the drug in my system. Despite my dependency, Julius and I had chemistry together. He started to grow very fond of me, and I always thought he was the most handsome man alive. One night when I was feigning for my medicine he refused to supply me. He said no more drugs for both of us. He forced me into detox and came to see me every day. Julius never left my side. He even agreed to stop selling drugs if I would get myself clean and be with him permanently. No one had ever thought much about me, not even my family during my collapse. I was too much of an embarrassment to the church. I accepted Julius offer and managed to get myself clean. He also wanted to live a different lifestyle for himself. Julius became disgusted with how he was poisoning his people, so he declined to sell anymore drugs, which angered his supplier.

When the time came for us to be together, Julius was arrested for possession to sell. He was sent away for three years. I never heard from him again until three years later. After his stint in prison he surprised me when he dropped by my parents church to say he wanted me to be his wife. I was single at the time and even if I wasn't, his looks would've made me leave whoever I was with. The chemistry between us had never died. It was challenging for him in the beginning to find work as an ex-con, but I pulled some strings and he was hired with the Baltimore transit. It's difficult for me not to think about him. We shared so many wonderful times together. Why did he have to do this to me, and with my friend? I'm trying to be tough by telling myself I don't need him, but who am I kidding? I need this man! And if I don't get him back soon enough I will have a nervous breakdown. I don't care what my family says about his character. He was there for me when they had just about buried me. I miss his touch. I miss his warmth. And I miss his handsome features. It's either him or resort back to using drugs, because I can't do this alone. Forgive me God. Strike the last sentence away from my heart and help me to rely on you instead of my own understanding. Help me lord through my torment and give me strength to overcome.

I have to place my attention on something else besides Julius. My apartment feels empty without him. I stretch out on the sofa and stare at the blank television screen. Normally, Julius and I would be watching Martin at this time, laughing hysterically. I'm in no mood to watch anything or do anything. I just want to sit here in my misery and be left alone. I adjust my sofa pillow and close my eyes. Five minutes into my relaxation, the cell rings. I reach down to get my phone off the hardwood floor. My heart sinks a little. I thought it might be Julius, but instead, it's Gertrude.

"Hi Gertrude, how can I help you?" I ask forcing enthusiasm in my tone of voice.

"I was just calling to check up on you. How are you holding up?"

"I'm lying on my sofa in the dark staring into space."

"Do you need anything?"

"No Gertrude. You have done more than enough for me already. I don't want to impose on you any further."

"Have you checked the files yet?"

"Oh my God Gertrude, It never even crossed my mind. I've been distracted with other things. Thanks for reminding me. I will call you back when I have something."

"Ok Ms. M. Goodbye."

I get up off the sofa as soon as I end the call with Gertrude and turn on the lamp. My briefcase is in the corner sitting next to the entertainment center. I grab my briefcase returning back to the cream color leather sofa. I'm thankful she awakened me out of my stupor. The fact I've have been fired should be my main concern instead of worrying about Julius and his unfaithfulness. This is exactly what I need to delve into so I can shift my emphasis away from him. I remove the report out of my briefcase and begin searching for inconsistencies. Everything looks good so far to my disappointment. I continue to thoroughly check the names inside the report. The payments from each loan recipient is accruing interest and up to date. Their names are abbreviated in capital letters with the loan amount and payment information next to each candidate's name. I'm halfway through the report and I don't see anything that will raise an eyebrow. It looks like my job will be history along with my relationship with Julius. This report appears to be no different than the ledger I was trying to balance. Gertrude gave a valiant effort, and I will give her that. She did some amazing work to get this report to me as a secretary, nonetheless there's nothing in it to go on. The personal loans are located at the top of the report and the business loans are at the bottom. I've scanned every personal loan to date, there's simply nothing that stands out. I'm almost finished with the business loans, a third of the way completed when three abbreviated letters jump out at me. M.O.M. I don't recall ever viewing this business name inside the ledger. I glance over at the loan payments and there aren't any. But instead, payments are being paid out to this company. I check the payment history and nearly fall off the sofa. This company has been receiving funds from us for years in altered amounts. There's a recent payment in amount of five thousand dollars just last month, and another for the amount of four thousand dollars a month before that. It goes on and on and on. How is it that I overlooked this account?

I'm not blind. I have perfect 20/20 vision. If this account was active this long, I would've noticed it. It was deliberately hidden from me. I think Thomas and I need to have a talk right away. If he doesn't want to see me then I will go to him. Fired or not. I call Gertrude right away to share the information with her. Her voicemail comes on and I leave her a brief message. I'm excited from what I just discovered. I will have a chance to get my job back. Mr. Pearson will be impressed with my finding. I turn off the lamp getting comfortable on the sofa feeling satisfied. It's still pretty early, but I don't have any desire to stay up. I haven't slept in the bedroom since Julius's infidelity. Lying alone without him being next to me will bring back painful memories, so I choose to sleep on the sofa instead. I adjust the sofa pillow behind my head curling up to get comfortable. My cell phone chimes again. I know its Gertrude. I reach for the phone and turn on my lamp. The number displayed is a private number. Who the heck is calling me private? It has to be Julius. I know it's him. My heart races with the thought of hearing his voice. Is he calling to apologize? And if he is, will I accept his apology? I honestly miss him, and I need him to come back to me. We have something extraordinary that Jodie can never take away with just sex. It takes more than that to keep a man. She can't even cook. If he stays with her he will starve to death.

"Hello?"

"Maya, this is Jodie." *Speak of the devil; I can't believe this woman is calling my phone after what she's done to me. She's literally insane. I hate her to the core.*

"If you're looking for Julius he's not here. As a matter of fact, you should know where he is. Isn't he supposed to be with you right now? I don't know why you're calling me."

"Why would I want Julius when I have Jeffrey? I'm engaged to your brother." *Not much longer, if I can help it.*

"Stop lying to me Jodie. I know you're fucking Julius. You're nothing but a whore, a dirty piece of white trash."

"I didn't call to argue with you. We can finish this conversation when it's more appropriate." *She's not running things, I am. She may control Julius and Jeffrey but she won't dictate to me.*

"The time is perfect for me. I have nothing else to do."

"It's about your brother." *What has she done now?*

"What about my brother? What have you done to him?"

"Maya, before you get your panties in a bunch. I haven't done anything to him. We were both in a car accident and Jeffrey has suffered a severe head injury causing him to lose his memory." *Oh my God.*

"I told him to leave you alone. Who was driving the car?"

"That doesn't matter."

"It does matter. Who was driving the car?"

"I was, but that's irrelevant."

"It's not irrelevant. You probably tried to kill him." *She cannot tell me otherwise. I'm no fool.*

CHAPTER 19

JEFFREY

Two African American women enter my hospital room. I search their faces for any identifiable marks which might jot my memory concerning their identity. Their faces are clear of any such thing. The older woman is wearing a flowered colored sun dress. Her hair or I believe her black wig is neatly cropped on her head with an arrangement of dazzling curls. The small wrinkles surrounding her brown eyes and the sagging skin underneath her neck give away her age. I would guess she is somewhere between fifty and sixty years of age. There's a certain confidence about her. Her chin is held high as if she's royalty. The woman standing beside her dressed in biker shorts and a tank top slightly resembles the older woman. She's young, very fit and beautiful. And her hazel eyes portray a hint of unhappiness. The outline of her mouth and nose is formed exactly like the older woman. Mother and daughter, and I presume I am the son.

"Jeffrey, I am your mother. My name is Wanita. And this is your sister Maya. I know you don't remember much of anything in the past. We're here to take you home.

"Where is the woman that told me she was my fiancée? She was here earlier. She never left my side."

"When we arrived here Jeffrey we didn't see a woman. Are you sure there was a woman here with you?" *I may have lost my long-term memory, but my short-term memory is in fine working order. I know she was here. Her face was simply too beautiful to forget.*

"Wanita, I know what I saw. You can ask the doctor. He even spoke with her."

"I'm afraid not Jeffrey. I've already spoken with him. He said no one has been here besides us."

"How can that be?" *I'm not thinking irrational. I saw her with my own two eyes. I know I did.*

"Jeffrey, you suffered a major head injury. It's more than likely you've been hallucinating."

"I'm not hallucinating Maya. Go get the doctor so I can ask him! I will prove it to you. *Explaining there was a woman in my room with me is causing my head to further throb even harder. Wanita comes back with the doctor. The doctor looks Jewish. He's tall and thin with black curly hair.*

"Jeffrey, do you have a question for me? And how is your head feeling?" *In agony, I press my fingers in a circular motion against my temples.*

"It's awful. I need something stronger to take for this pain."

"I'll write out a new prescription before you leave; something a little more potent. It should help alleviate the sharp pain you're feeling."

"Do you remember the woman that was here in the room with me?" I ask the doctor.

"There hasn't been anyone in the room with you besides a nurse. I've been checking on you every so often. Are you certain there was someone here with you?" *There had to be, unless I dreamt it. But, it was too real to be a dream. She stayed by my side the entire time. She told me she was my fiancée. I heard her loud and clear. It wasn't a dream. I know it wasn't.*

"Doctor, are you positively sure there wasn't anyone here?"

"Not of my knowledge."

"What about the nurse? She had to see her."

"I questioned the nurse. She said you were alone in the room." *I have a hunch the three of them are lying to me. Why would they lie? It doesn't make sense. Why lie to me about Jodie not ever being here? Are these two women actually from my family? And if so, why don't they believe me? Wouldn't they like to see me happy? I'm unable to remember my past, but I'm longing to know my future starting with the woman that came to visit me.*

"The three of you think I'm delusional, like I'm making this up? The woman was here with me. The three of you can't tell me otherwise."

"Jeffrey, you need not worry yourself over this. The most important thing for you to do right now is to take it easy."

"Your mother is right Jeffrey. You just had a harrowing experience and you're lucky to be alive. Try to relax yourself and remain calm. You need all the rest you can get right now. In time everything will come back to you. Maybe, even the woman you're referring to."

"I don't even remember what happened to me. Can you tell me exactly what took place?"

"You were in a car accident, an eighteen wheeler rammed into you from behind."

"Was I driving or was I a passenger?" *Wanita quickly interrupts the doctor.*

"You were driving honey. The scene was awful. Your car was pushed several feet in the air flipping over a few times. It was on the news. Other motorists helped you to get out of your car before calling 911. The fact that you're here is nothing but God's grace."

"Was I alone inside the vehicle?"

"Yes you were."

"What made the truck driver run into me?"

"There are several reports stating the driver was intoxicated at the time of the crash. The state police discovered beer cans inside his rig. The driver was a recovering alcoholic for several years. Something on that particular day caused him to snap ending his sobriety."

"Well, I guess I'm ready to go home, wherever that is."

"Jeffrey, I have advised your mother to let you stay with her until your memory fully expands. It is very important you have someone looking after you."

"How long will I suffer from memory loss?"

"With memory loss we can never really say when you will fully recover. In some instances it can take a week, a couple of months, or even a day. It depends on how you process information and how you come to recognize subtle cues in your familiar environment. I will definitely stay in contact with you to check on your progress. Remember to take care of yourself and no strenuous activities. Relaxation is the key. And one more thing, try not to think too much about what you can't recall. It will come back to you in due time. Let it happen naturally."

Outside the hospital the sun is beaming with intensity. It's a beautiful day, but nothing in comparison to the attractive woman who came to visit me. Not for once do I believe the doctor or my so called mother and sister. Jodie touched my hand feeling comfortable in my presence. I saw the affection radiating from her bright green eyes. If only I could experience the same feeling of knowing her. How would it feel to love her, or to make love to her? I need to know. I have to know. And I will search for Jodie until I find her. No one will stop me from finding out the truth. Why would a woman as beautiful as her tell me she's my fiancée? She can have any man alive with minimal effort. A woman of her degree has no reason to lie. If she said were engaged it must be true, but why are these two women in the front of the car lying to me? If she isn't my woman than who is? Or am I divorced? Or maybe I'm single. I don't feel like I'm single or divorced. I know I have someone to love. I can just feel it.

"Jeffrey, are you comfortable back there?"

"I certainly am Wanita. I like how this car handles. It's very smooth on the bumps."

"Jeffrey, I know it's early in your recovery process. But, don't you think it's better to call me mom instead of Wanita?" *I would give into her suggestion if I felt the motherly love from her, but I don't. I feel nothing from either of them.*

"I will try. It's just not there. It's like I'm pretending if I say it."

"I don't mind if you pretend. Just hearing the word mom coming from your mouth signifies to me that I'm your mother instead of a stranger."

"Ok, I can see where that might be a problem for you. I will give it my best effort to say mom from now on," *she smiles at me through the rearview mirror and then turns her attention back to the road in front of her. I hope my memory returns soon. I need to know the truth. I need know who Jodie really is. And from the looks of things, I'm positive Wanita and Maya will continue to lie to me.*

CHAPTER 20

JULIUS

"I'm sorry for what I've done to you Maya. If you give me another chance I promise I will do better. I miss you so much. I will never hurt you again the way that I have. You can count on it. My heart bleeds for you."

"Do you love her Julius?"

"No, that's just it. I don't love her. I only love you, and my love for you hasn't changed since the first time we met. I know it doesn't look that way by my actions, but no one can replace you. I mean that."

"Then, why Julius? Why did you have to sleep with her? You knew she was my friend, and you betrayed me anyway. How can you say you love me and do something like this to me? I want to believe in you, but how do I know if you're telling me the truth or not? How do I know you won't hurt me again if I allow you back into my life?"

"Haven't I been there for you through thick and thin? I was the one who turned you away from drugs. Your family didn't care about you. Everyone left you out there to die, except me. Even though you were hooked on drugs I saw a special quality in you. I knew underneath your addiction mask a beautiful, intelligent, and vibrant woman existed. I had to uncover the exterior to find you, and once I did I never looked back."

"Why must you constantly bring up my drug addiction when trying to make a point? If I'm not mistaken, wasn't it you that sold the drugs to me in the first place? You were part of the reason for my plight. So don't pretend like you've done so much for me. As I recall very clearly, you almost killed me by giving me the drugs."

"I know I gave the drugs to you. I also stopped giving them to you. I quit selling them, and I did everything in my power to make amends for crippling half the neighborhood."

"That's one of the things I can't wrap my brain around. You know how bad my addiction once was, so why betray me? Why would you sleep with my friend when you know I'm a recovering addict? I don't need this type of pressure in my life."

"I will not bring you anymore added pressure. I'm here to love you and nothing's changed. I would like to get married. Don't forget we have a wedding to attend to. The invitations have been mailed out. A hall has been rented and payed for and our family and friends are looking forward to it."

"How can you speak of a wedding with what you've done to me? Do you expect me to walk up to an altar and marry you when everyone inside the church will know you cheated on me? First, I will look like a fool. And secondly, my family will not accept it."

"The only information your family has to go on is what you tell them. There's no proof, only you and I know what really happened."

"If you're suggesting I lie to my family I will not do it."

"Maya, do you still love me?"

"I've never stopped loving you Julius. However, the hurt won't go away. I need time to think."

"How much time?"

"I can't say. I need to be certain you will not cheat on me again. As of now I just don't know. It will take some time for me to trust you again."

"Don't you believe me?"

"I do believe you, but actions speak louder than words."

I spent most of my half hour break trying to convince Maya to take me back. I know I put her through some stuff. If she gives me another chance I will not disappoint her. I meant every single word I said to her over the phone. I definitely want her back in my life, and I will do all I need to do to get her back. She is the most important thing to me right now. I'm done with that crazy white woman. My focus will be on Maya from here on out. She will come around in a matter of time. I just have to be patient. This is my first day back to work since the scene that took place inside the church. The rest gave me time to think. I know for a fact Jodie is not the person I want to spend the rest of my life with. She doesn't even come close to being on Maya's level. I don't know what I was thinking. As I head further down Crenshaw Avenue I realize Benny's voice is absent from my ears. My ears would be bleeding right now if he was riding the bus. I'm sorry for how I bullied him in front of Maya and also in front of Jodie. It wasn't his fault. I lost a good friend due to my selfishness. The stop ahead is pretty crowded. There are about six people waiting for the bus. I pull up to the curb and open the door letting them in one by one as they pay their bus fare to ride. I didn't notice him standing behind the other passengers, but the last person to board the bus is a man I don't care to see. He gets on the bus sitting in the seat Benny usually occupies. I wonder what kind of scheme his ass is up to now. I threw away important years of my life getting involved with him.

"The great Julius Miles, what an honor. Does everyone on this bus realize they're in the presence of greatness? Can we please get your autograph, Mr. Basketball? *He's still the same annoying bastard. Somethings never change.*

"Fuck you Darius. I'm not in the mood for your games. What the hell do you want?"

"Is that how you greet a friend?"

"Show me a friend and I will greet him like one," *my response disturbs him. It ruffles his feathers a bit as his cool expression hardens.*

"As I recall Julius, I'm the one that got you started making money when your basketball career ended abruptly. What a waste to have all the skills you acquired over the years along with your athletic ability. To simply have it thrown away in an instant is a tragedy. Young boys can only dream about having your God given six foot four frame and talent. How does it feel to know a woman is the reason for you losing everything?"

"Enough already Darius, what is the real reason for this intrusion?

"Calm down Julius, this will only take a minute of your time. Do you remember when you were arrested?"

"How can I ever forget? The feds stole three years of my life. I didn't give them any information. I'm no snitch. I did my time without complaining."

"I can respect that. You held it down for all of us, nevertheless there are some loose ends."

"What the hell are you talking about? That life is behind me. I'm a changed man. I don't sell poison to my people anymore."

"Some of that poison was confiscated by the feds. I'm out of twenty thousand large, and I need to collect."

"If you think I have twenty thousand large just lying around growing interest then you must be using your own drugs," *his round eyes constrict with indignation as I glare back at him in the rearview mirror.*

"Nigga, do you think this is a joke? I want all of my money you lost, and I mean every dime of it. I remember a time when you were one of the hardest niggas on the street. You let nothing come between you and the money. And then you got soft when you allowed that fine piece of ass control your future. As a matter of fact, how is Maya?" *If I didn't need this job I would beat the hell out of him right now. I'm so close to losing my job. Let him keep it up.*

"Don't you ever say her name, you hear me?"

"Damn, someone's nose is wide open. Does she still have that nice rounded ass? Remember how we all used to go crazy for her? It's a shame how she became strung out though. Who would have ever thought it, an educated girl strung out on heroin. That girl did anything to get her drug of choice. I heard so many stories," *If his high yellow ass says one more thing to upset me, I will do what I gotta do. I'm no punk. And he knows how I get down.*

"Just close your mouth about her Darius before I put you out myself."

"Testy, testy, I tell you what J; I will put it like this. Your main problem to begin with is women. You let a married white woman destroy your basketball career when you had to jump out of her bedroom window upon her husband returning home, and tore your damn ACL. Then, you quit selling drugs for me because you fell for another woman. You went to jail because you got soft. That's how you lost my money Julius. I'm giving you a month. That's all you got."

"I can't come up with that kind of money and you know it."

"Well, you better think of something, or I just might have to give Maya a visit. You know what they say, once an addict always an addict." *If he touches her, he's dead.*

"Did you forget who I am Darius? Don't let this bus uniform deceive you. If you take it there all hell will break loose. I can promise you that, partner."

"Julius, you don't scare me. The old Julius would've pounced on me already for making threats. You've gotten soft."

"It's not about being soft; it's about being smart. I need this job. If I hit you I will definitely lose my job."

"How sad Mr. bus driver. You were doing well working for me, and now your ass is working for pennies. You're nothing but a joke. I expect to have my money in a month, no exceptions." *Some of the passengers get up from their seats to exit the bus as I open the service door. Darius exits with them. He has me seething inside. One thing I know about Darius is when he says something he usually follows through. He was raised in the streets. I have to prepare myself for the worse possible scenario.*

CHAPTER 21

JODIE

I presume I'm out of Jeffrey's life until he fully regains his long term memory. I pray to God it comes back to him soon enough before he forgets me entirely. My intuition is telling me his mother and sister are working together to get rid of me. What will I do without Jeffrey being around? He's an important part of my life. I will just have to force my way over there to see him, even if it means getting into trouble. If they think for a minute I will not fight for my man then the both of those biddies are dreaming. I suggest the two of them wake up and smell the coffee. He will remember me whether they have a say in it or not. Maybe if I reach out to Julius he can help me. I know he's not fond of Jeffrey, but if I explain the facts to him he just might agree. What can it hurt to try? I will go the extra mile for Jeffrey, and I'm positive he would do the same for me. I should be working at the moment, on the other hand how can I work when I can't stop thinking about Jeffrey? I wonder what he's doing at this moment. Is he safe? Does he have the proper care? Or better yet, what are his mother and sister up to? He didn't even recognize me after the accident. He had no recollection of us ever being together. I'm still in shock. We had something special together, and a stupid truck driver took it away from us in a matter of seconds. I need to call Julius right away. I have to know how my baby is doing in the hands of his mother and sister. I punch in his number. The phone rings five times before he answers.

"Hello?"

"Julius?"

"This is Julius. Who is this?"

"This is Jodie. We need to talk."

"Are you slow? Did your mother drop you on your head at birth?"

"Excuse me?"

"I didn't stutter Jodie. I told you to stay away from me. Do you want me to call the police and tell them you're harassing me?"

"How am I harassing you?"

"Look woman, I'm tired of your mess. I don't ever want to see your face again. Stay the hell away from me. There's something extremely wrong with you. You definitely need to see a doctor. You have a serious problem and I can't help you."

"Are you acting this way because of Maya?"

"Without a doubt, but don't get me wrong. I deserve just as much as blame as you."

"I don't get it Julius. But never mind that. I need a favor from you."

"If I do you this favor will you finally leave me the hell alone?" *He is really out there. Poor guy.*

"Yes. If that's what you want?"

"It's definitely what I want."

"I understand Julius."

"Are you sure you will stay away from me then?"

"I promise."

"Ok, what's the favor?"

"It's Jeffrey. He's been in an accident."

"What kind of accident?"

"He was involved in a car accident. A tractor trailer struck him from the rear and now he can't remember a thing, total amnesia. He doesn't remember anyone, not even me."

"Damn, talk about bad luck. I would say I feel for the brother, but I don't have an ounce of pity for him."

"I'm not asking for your pity Julius. I need your help in reaching him. Maya and her mother are taking care of him. He needs twenty-four hour care. There's no way possible for me to speak with Jeffrey while your fiancée and her mother are in the house with him."

"I see what you mean. The both of us are at the top of Maya's shit list. I don't know which one she hates more, you or me?"

"She probably hates both of us on the same level."

"When you showed up at the church to see Benny's baptism it really pushed her over the edge, don't you think?" *Benny's baptism? Who the heck is Benny? And why would I attend his baptism?*

"I know, maybe I shouldn't have done that?"

"You think? She had a fit. I don't know why you had to flirt with him? Wasn't it enough you had my full attention? You didn't have to include Benny. The poor guy is hopeless. I know you did it to get me jealous when I told you we were done. On top of it, Benny told Maya about us. That's when I lost it. I knocked him out inside the sanctuary. Her brothers chased me out of the church. I barely got out of there." *My sister is up to her same old antics. God help us all.*

"I don't know what to say."

"Have you heard from Benny?"

"No, I haven't".

"I hope the brother is ok."

"Will you be able to help me then?"

"I'm slowly working my way back into her life. She's at least talking to me. I think she misses me. I know I miss her."

"So, you think Maya will absolutely forgive you?" *How could you do this to her? She loves you entirely. If I didn't need Jeffrey I would have nothing to do with you at all. You conniving bastard.*

"I think in time she will, if I play my cards right."

"What about her family? Especially her father, he's a pastor."

"No one besides Maya knows exactly what you and I did together. I think she'll bend the truth some." *Correction; what you and Julia did together. Leave me out of it.*

"How do you know that? If she reacted like you say she did inside the church, her family will all the more believe you did something terrible to her. In addition to that, you fled the church after hitting someone which makes you look guilty. I'm sure Maya spilled her guts out to everyone after she found out about you and me. Now you assume she will convince her family that all is well between you two?" Her brothers definitely won't buy it, or her so called righteous mother."

"She will have to make them believe if we are to get married." *He still expects Maya to marry him? Is he delusional? How do you marry an unfaithful man?*

"That I'm afraid will be a difficult task, especially if you're planning to get married in her parent's church."

"Nothing's impossible with God." *If you knew God you wouldn't've cheated on your fiancée.*

"How will you help me get to Jeffrey?"

"My agenda as of now will consist of doing everything I can to convince Maya I'm serious about her. It will take her some time to put her guard down. I really screwed up. I should have never touched you. I'm trying to do better. I really don't know if she will take me back or not. If things work out as planned, and I'm able to get her back, I will definitely see to it you're reunited with Jeffrey." *You should've never touched my sister. I wonder what she has instore for you. Oh, you will surely pay for what you have done to Maya.*

"I need to get to him ASAP. The longer I'm away from him the quicker he will forget about me. I can only imagine what they have concocted to keep me out of the picture."

"Maybe it's nothing."

"It's something, believe me. Whatever it is, I need you to find out and get back to me."

"I will, as long as you stay away from me."

"I told you. It's a done deal. I will leave you alone." *But, Julia will not.*

"Ok. I'll call you soon. Bye"

"Bye". *I will not sit idle and wait for Julius to help me. My time is running out, especially with my sister running loose. I will jumpstart the mission on my own, starting today. What can it hurt to drive down his mother's street?*

CHAPTER 22

MAYA

My mother decided to bring Jeffrey to my brother's place before setting him up in her home. We need time to rearrange the scenery with pictures of Vanessa Spellman. As soon as we arrive to Michael's house she talks with his wife to get her sister over at once. She also informs her to make certain her sister brings as many pictures of herself as possible. If Jeffrey can get a visual of Vanessa in action it may allow us to promote her as his girlfriend. Michael walks into the living room.

"Maya, what are you and mom up to now?"

"We have to get Jeffrey away from Jodie. She's not right for him Michael."

"And how do you plan on doing that when he's in love with her?"

"By introducing Vanessa as his girlfriend, it's perfect. With his loss of memory he will not question it."

"How can mom being the first lady of the church do such devilish things? Does dad know about this?" He shakes his head in disgust.

"Dad doesn't know anything, and you better not tell him. We have to do this Michael. Jodie is bad news."

"I don't understand this? Why all the hatred against Jodie now? The two of you were college roommates and the best of friends."

"Jodie sleeps around Michael. She did it back in college, and she's continuing to do it. She's unfaithful."

"How do you know she's unfaithful to Jeffrey? Did he tell you this himself?"

"No, but she slept with someone I know. They told me everything," he looks stumped.

"I like Jodie. It doesn't sound like her to me. Are you sure this person is telling you the truth? Maybe their jealous as to what she and Jeffrey have together. People will spread all kinds of gossip to break up a solid relationship. You can't just trust hearsay."

"It's not hearsay its factual evidence."

"I know one thing; I won't be a part of this mess. When his memory returns and he finds out the truth, he will not be a happy camper. He will look for someone to blame."

"What if his memory never fully returns?"

"It will return, trust me."

"How do you know that?"

"I just know. He won't be in the dark forever." The sound of Michael's doorbell interrupts us. My mother sprints through the house like at track star to greet Vanessa at the door. Vanessa walks inside the living room accompanied by my mother and Michael's wife Gloria.

"The four of you have got to be kidding me right?"

"Lower you voice Michael, Jeffrey might hear you," my mother warns.

"He should hear everything because this isn't the right thing to do. All of you should be ashamed of yourselves. Like I told Maya a few minutes ago, I will not be a part of this lie."

"Michael, that woman is playing him for a fool. I will not allow any of my children to be swindled by anyone. I'm sick of her kind anyway, always getting what they want."

"Mama, you're being racist."

"I'm not being racist. I'm only stating the facts. It is what it is. When a good job comes along they're the first to get it, and when a good black man comes along they're the first to get them too."

"Gloria, are you coming with me? I'm leaving. I can't stick around and listen to this anymore."

"Michael, I think what your mother and sister are attempting to do is the right thing. As black women we need to stick together and support one another when it comes to saving our black men. I'm staying put. You can leave if you want to," Michael leaves the living room heading for the front door. Gloria tells us she and Vanessa are down for the cause. Vanessa and Gloria favor each other. The two sisters have high cheek bones and oriented coffee colored eyes.

"I brought as many pictures as I could. I hope it works," Vanessa says.

"It will work, as long as the four of us work together on this. Remember, he doesn't know a thing about his past. We have to create one for him. If we do this right he will never see that woman again."

"There aren't any pictures of Jeffrey and me together. Do you think he will question it?" Vanessa asks.

"Knowing my brother, he probably will. If he questions you later on about it just tell him he hates taking pictures, which really isn't that far from the truth. He's camera shy."

"Ok, I will do my best to convince him."

"No. Your best isn't good enough Vanessa. You have to sell it to him. You have to make my son believe you're his girlfriend. Vanessa, I need you to pour your heart and soul into my son. He has to believe you mean the world to him. Love him completely. Overwhelm him. Do not let him up for air," Vanessa looks tentative after what my mother suggests.

"Are you sure you can pull this off Vanessa?"

"I'm positive. I've always had a thing for your brother, and I believe he's attracted to me. This is my opportunity to win Jeffrey over for good."

After we end our discussion my mother gathers the pictures from Vanessa and departs from Michael's home. I told her I would bring Jeffrey to her house in a couple of hours. It will give her time to organize Vanessa's pictures inside of her home. I truly want this to work. The sooner he can connect with Vanessa the better the chances of him forgetting about Jodie entirely. I quietly open the door walking into my brother's spare bedroom where Jeffrey is sleeping soundly. I wonder how long will it take for him to get accustomed to being with Vanessa. I pray to God it happens as quickly as possible. It's time to put our plan into action. I gently tap Jeffrey to wake him. He slowly turns over on his right side and begins to open his eyes.

"Hey brother, how do you feel?"

"I feel like I've been in a train wreck. My head is still throbbing and my body is aching," he sits up to stretch.

"Jeffrey, it was nothing but the grace of God that spared your life. There's no way else to explain it. I'm so happy he did. I would've lost it if anything happened to you, and I know Vanessa would've felt exactly the same way."

"Vanessa? Who's Vanessa?"

"She's your girlfriend."

"I have a girlfriend?" He scratches his head.

"Of course you do. She's in the living room waiting to see you."

"I don't have any recollection of ever having a girlfriend. Forgive me for asking, is she pretty?"

"You'll have to see for yourself. Are you ready to meet her?"

"Yes I am. I have to learn more about my past to be able to know where I'm going in the future."

When Jeffrey and I enter the living room Vanessa is sitting comfortably on the couch. Her natural black hair is styled in a triple twist up-do. She is dressed in white shorts revealing a lot of leg and has on a white tank top along with a pair of white sketchers. Jeffrey is drawn to Vanessa immediately as his eyes appear fixated on her. She gets up from the couch rushing over to give him a warm hug. Vanessa pours on the act which looks convincing to me.

"Honey, I'm so glad you're ok. I was a nervous wreck when they told me about your accident. If anything had happened to you I don't know what I would've done without you. I love you so much," she kisses his lips. Jeffrey hesitantly raps his arms around her.

As I continue to watch Vanessa display her Oscar winning theatrics in front of my brother, I am amazed at how unambiguous she seems. My brother is holding onto every word she declares. He's connecting with her as I begin to see a sparkle in his eyes. Vanessa is a beautiful woman by far, and I believe her attractiveness is making her act much more convincing. Men find beautiful women irresistible. Their senses are often clouded when striking looks are involved. At this very moment Jeffrey is being pulled in by an imposter. The things women can do to men are astonishing. Females have an abundance of power over men. If Vanessa can pull this off completely, Jodie will be a thing of the past. I leave the living room allowing the two of them to get better aquatinted with each other. I've taken care of one of three things on my agenda. The first was Jeffrey, the second is getting my job back, and the third is working on my relationship with Julius. At least I have the first one partly completed. The second and third will be just as much if not even more difficult to accomplish. I know for a fact Thomas is hiding something from me. He's avoided me long enough. It's time for us to meet head on. I need answers, and I will force him to provide them if he refuses. As crazy as it sounds, I still have a soft spot for Julius. I can't get this man out of my mind. Is it so wrong to give a person a second chance? What if he hurts me again? I don't know if I can bare it a second time, nonetheless I still love him.

CHAPTER 23

JEFFREY

What type of man has a wife-to-be and a girlfriend at the same time? As stunning as Vanessa truly is, the woman at the hospital is by far more beautiful. I'm convinced Jodie is my fiancée. Why would she arrive at the hospital and say those things to me if they weren't true? It just doesn't make any sense to me, no matter what my mother and sister implies. With all that being said, Vanessa is crazy for me. She worships the ground I walk on. She caters to my every need. She smothers me with her affection. And to tell you the truth, I am definitely enjoying every single moment of it. Vanessa told me I was introduced to her through her sister, which is my brother's wife. She is perfect for me in every sense of the word. The only drawback I have is her annoying high-pitched tone of voice. It's definitely a turnoff sometimes, but I guess I can get used to it. Vanessa knows so much about me. I asked her question after question and she answered them all without uncertainty. She told me that my father founded Shiloh Baptist Ministries and constructed the church with his very own money. Before my father became a pastor, he played the numbers literally every day of the week. He believed like everyone else his dollar and a dream would change his life forever. It so happens, his dollar and a dream became true when he won the mega millions for three million dollars after taxes. Vanessa said my father had visions of pastoring a church when he served on the deacon board for many years at his local church. The money afforded him the opportunity to enroll in divinity school and learn everything he could about religion and pastoring.

After he received his numerous degrees he started looking for an area to construct his building. When he found what he was looking for he purchased the land and created Shiloh Baptist Ministries. I also learned I'm a CEO of a prominent software company. I'm learning more and more about my life and those important to me. I'm still having trouble remembering my past. The doctor said it will take some time to get back to the old me. As of now I'm enjoying the discovery process of my life. I can honestly say my life is looking pretty good at the moment. If I had one thing to complain about as of now it would be the fact I have to live with my parents instead of living on my own. I would like to see the place where I live. It may jolt my memory and help me to regain my past. If only I could remember the things in my past I wouldn't need their support. I'm beginning to feel like a prisoner amongst them. I need to find out more about myself. It seems to me that my mother and sister are unwilling to show me. I've been staying at my parents place for about a week. My mother has notified the software company with regards to my loss of memory. There giving me time to get myself together. I haven't spoken with anyone except Vanessa. I asked my mother where my friends are. She said I don't have many friends and I sort of stick to myself, and the few friends I do have live in other states. I assume if I have friends there must be a way to reach them. So, I asked my mother for the contact information. She explained I lost my phone during the car accident and she has no way of finding out the telephone numbers. I can sense she's lying to me. Why doesn't she let me find out more about myself? She's deliberately keeping my in the dark. I think it's time for me to take actions with or without them. I consider today is the perfect day to start my reawakening process.

I don't remember anything about my parent's neighborhood except what Vanessa shared with me. She claimed my sister and I roamed this area as children. Come to think of it, it's perplexing how Vanessa can recall every detail about my life. We're not even married and she knows anything and everything about the trivial things in my past. When it comes to her providing solid information to assist me in remembering who I am she doesn't know much. It's as if she's been briefed beforehand. If she loves me as much as she says then why won't she help me? I need to know who I am, and I need to know now. I don't have much time before everyone comes home. As I look around my parent's massive dwelling I am impressed to say the least. They have everything a home should have and more. Their taste in the finer things is evident throughout the home. The furniture, kitchen *appliances, and fashionable interior of the home are without a question top of the line.*

Their six bedroom Georgian style home sits profoundly on a 5 acre ranch. My parents have livestock on their property. When my father won the lottery he moved away as far from the city as possible. There isn't a store or gas station for miles. As I step outside the sun greets me with contempt. The heat from the sun scorches my skin. I close my parent's gate and start my Journey down the extensive never ending road. The majority of the homes located on this road are similar in detail with an abundance of spacious land. I've been walking for thirty minutes now and I still haven't seen a store yet, but I do see a car approaching. The driver appears to be looking for a certain estate as they slow down at each residence. When the driver gets near me the car comes to a complete stop. I am unable see the driver through the tinted glass. The window comes down slowly. It's her, the woman from the hospital. I would recognize her beautiful face from anywhere.

"Do you need a ride handsome?" She smiles showing her pearly whites.

"My mother warned me to never get in a car with strangers, but I think in this case I'll make an exception," I open the car door and get inside. "This feels so much better than being out there."

"Smart choice. So why are you walking alone in this heat?"

"I need to find out some answers about who I am."

"I'm sure I can assist you in that area if you allow me to."

"I need all the help I can get. How much do you know about me?

"I know enough to help you get your memory back. I definitely know where you live and where you work. Would you like me to take you there?"

"Yes I would. Before we go, can I ask you something that's been bothering me?"

"Go right ahead. I'm here to help."

"Are you really my fiancé?"

"That I am. Here's the ring to prove it. I know you don't remember purchasing it, but you bought it for me."

"If that's true why are there pictures of Vanessa all over my parent's home? She says she's my fiancée. My family is telling me the same thing."

"Vanessa, Michael's wife sister is pretending to be your fiancé?"

"So, it isn't true?"

"It's definitely not true. She's lying. They're all liars. There's no validity to any of it."

"Why would they lie to me? What are they getting out of it?"

"It's me Jeffrey. The lie is set up to keep you away from me. Your mother and sister are not very fond of me being with you. As a matter of fact they hate my guts."

"Why do they dislike you?"

"Your sister doesn't believe I'm any good for you. She thinks I'm out to harm you. And your mother is a racist. She doesn't want you with a white woman."

"They must really dislike you to go so far as putting this charade together."

"You have no idea."

"If Vanessa is pretending she's one hell of an actor. The woman cooks like a chef. She prepares all of my favorite dishes and we get along so swell. She doesn't complain about anything. If I yell at her she apologizes for upsetting me. I've never seen her lose her composure."

"There you have it Jeffrey, it's just too perfect. What woman doesn't get upset from time to time? Every one of us loses our cool when the right buttons are pressed. She's cooking, cleaning, and apologizing for upsetting you? It sounds to me like you're King Arthur and she is your servant. The real Vanessa is hiding under the exterior your mother and sister built for her. I bet if you penetrate it just a little you will see the real person underneath it. How long can she actually hold up pretending to be someone she isn't?"

"I don't know, but she's damn good at it."

"What about the sex?"

"She allows me to do whatever I want, as long as she satisfies me," *Jodie's face turns bright red. I shouldn't have told her. I'm upsetting her.*

"I can't believe them! She's fucking you! And you're eating out the palm of her hand! Jeffrey, you have to get your memory back. I need you to know the truth. This is not fair to me. I love you. You need to wake up. I can't sit idle and allow them to manipulate your life. Something has to be done at once!" *Jodie drops her head against the steering wheel. She turns her head toward the driver's window. I place my hand on her back.*

"I'm sorry for hurting you. I feel terrible I can't remember a thing about our past. It's like I've never met you before, except at the hospital. I have no recollection of us ever being together. Although, you are truly a beautiful woman, a man would have to be blind not to notice."

"What about a kiss? A kiss may bring your memory back." *I thought she would never ask. I've been dying to kiss her.*

"Yes, I would like that very much."

"Well handsome, these lips are all yours. Pucker up." *I remove the strands of hair covering her face as I gaze into her moist green eyes. I use my fingers and wipe the tears from her eyelids. I gently press my lips against hers as she responds by opening her mouth wider. Our tongues explore the satisfying warmth generated through our passionate kiss. She is pilfering my oxygen as I in return am engulfing hers. I close my eyes to enjoy the moment while trying earnestly to remember her. But nothing in my cognizance will appear. She's unfamiliar to me. As our kissing becomes more intense, my mind is filled with thoughts of Vanessa. Is she really pretending? Is this all a setup to get rid of Jodie? How can Jodie be so wrong for me when our passion for each other feels so right? I am confused to say the least. I need to find out the truth. One of them is lying to me. I will find out one way or another.*

CHAPTER 24

JULIUS

Our wedding day is just around the corner. I have a week to get my act together and convince Maya I still love her. I don't want to call off this wedding. We've put a great deal of planning into this day. I've lost so much by not thinking clearly over the years. Haven't I learned from my previous mistakes to keep my penis where it belongs? Seven years ago I was a high school basketball standout. I was sought after by every college in the country. They compared my basketball skills to Kolbe Bryant when he played high school ball. My six-foot four frame and feline quickness made it a challenge for defenders to guard me at the two guard position. I scored baskets at will. The game was so easy for me. I went through defenses and defenders effortlessly. My basketball IQ set me apart from the other players; it was as if I was a man playing among boys. During that time in my life I had chosen a university to continue my basketball career.

I signed a letter of intent to attend Georgetown University and was excited to get started, until I met Abigail Cohens. I was a freshman and Mrs. Abigail Cohens was my English professor. Professor Cohens attended every game and sat directly behind the team's bench. When I turned in essays she would never give me a grade lower than a B. I can write pretty well, but I knew for a fact some of my papers were not B material. I had misspelled words, run on sentences, and there were times when I just didn't put out my best effort, but my grade remained the same. And as always, she left her number on the bottom on the essay if I have any questions to call her. I never had a thing for older women. Mrs. Cohens was thirty-five and very attractive. When she taught her class she customarily dressed provocatively. All eyes were usually on her instead of the subject matter.

On a few occasions her husband would show up and bring her lunch for the day. He seemed like a very nice guy. He also taught at the university as a math professor. On the last paper I ever wrote in college, professor Cohens instructed me to come by her office for extra help. From the looks of my grades I couldn't figure out why I needed extra help. I had a solid B average. And as far as I could tell it was a waste of time to go visit her office. And besides, I had more important things to do. She didn't take kindly to my disregard and made it evident by issuing me a D grade on my following essay. At the bottom of my essay she demanded I attend her office for extra help or I would be repeating the class again next semester. I reluctantly made a visit to her office.

I knocked on her door and she kindly told me to have a seat. Pinned on the wall of her office was a doctorate degree in English from Yale University along with numerous teaching awards. There was a family photo of her with her husband and two children on top of the mahogany desk. Mrs. Cohen's level of sophistication oozed from her ombre color high slit maxi dress. Her large dark blue eyes traced my physique from head to toe. The red lipstick she wore accentuated her pale complexion along with her red layered shortened bobbed hairstyle. She seductively left her chair and sat on her desk directly in front of me crossing her well-formed thighs.

She grabbed a paper from her desk and handed it to me which displayed all of my stats since high school. Mrs. Cohen was a knowledgeable basketball fan and knew everything about me. She claimed she wanted to know what it would feel like to be seduced by a black athlete, because she was being sexually deprived at home. Her complaint stemmed from the fact her husband could not satisfy her. She said fifty seconds in the bedroom was not long enough. I said I couldn't help her until she forced my participation by threatening to fail me if I didn't cooperate. The way I saw it, I would be having my cake and eating it too. No matter what type of paper I wrote she would be passing me. This meant less time studying and more time to have fun while devouring her at the same time. What more could a college freshman ask for? For about a month it was going swell. Every Wednesday we would fuck each other like there was no tomorrow, and I was maintaining a 4.0 grade point average in English composition with minimal effort. But like all good things, they eventually come to an end. On that dreadful day as usual we met at her place. Her husband had a course to teach that morning. At least that's what the both of us assumed until he arrived early from calling out sick for the day. He pulled in the driveway while we were both in full eroticism. There was no time for me to do anything but jump out of the two story window to escape. The jump seemed short. I thought it would be a piece of cake to make. I was mistaken when I hit the ground and blew out my right knee. My collegiate basketball career ended in seconds. I left school entirely embarrassed by the incident. After surgery and about a year of rehabilitation, I tried to return to the court, but my knee was never the same again. I needed to find a job, and that's when I met Darius. I started selling drugs for him and made tons of money in the process. It wasn't NBA money, but it was the closest thing to it. He's a fool if he thinks I'm paying him a dime. I have money, lots of it, stashed away in a safe place. I realized back then the day would come when it all would end for me. I took the fall for all of their asses and did my time without opening my mouth. As far as I'm concerned the money is payback. I never meant to get Maya involved. She started hitting me up for drugs for fun and then she became addicted, just like that. Xavier introduced her to heroin. I deserve all the blame but at least she's clean now.

I seldom visit Maya at her job. I need to reach out to her. I've been calling her all day. If Darius is making threats I have to warn her. It may be a matter of life and death. I hate driving around in this economy rental car. My car insurance offered me this tight Toyota Yaris crap while my car is being fixed, thanks to Benny. The leg room sucks. I park in the visitor's parking lot and take the elevator up to the third floor. I ask the secretary for Maya. She looks at me bewildered like I'm crazy or something.

"Maya doesn't work here anymore," she tells me.

"What happened to her?"

"She was fired."

"Fired? Are you sure about that? Maya is a damn good accountant. Why would they fire her?"

"They're accusing her of stealing funds."

"How much funds are we talking about?"

"I really don't know the exact amount, but I heard it's in the thousands."

"Maya is not a thief. There has to be some mistake."

"If there is a mistake they haven't found it yet. I think they're about to press charges on her if she doesn't come up with the money very soon."

"She never mentioned it to me. I wonder why she didn't tell me."

"I don't know Julius, but she needs your help."

"I will help her. She's the love of my life. I will not let her go through this alone."

"I'm glad to hear that. She needs you now more than ever."

"I haven't been honest with her. I hurt her really bad, but I'm trying to change things. I just hope it isn't too late."

"If she loves you it's never too late. Whatever you did to her make sure you don't do it again. Be honest with her. I think everyone deserves another chance. I guess it's up to Maya."

Maya's secretary is exactly right. I have to be upfront with her from now on. She's everything I need. I will fight to keep her. My heart wants to believe Maya didn't take the missing funds, nevertheless my conscious is telling me she may have done it if she's using again. What if Darius has found her? His soul purpose would be to get back at me for not handing him his money. He would deliberately poison Maya with his drug paraphernalia because he's afraid of me. Darius would do anything to get back at me. He would send his punk ass goons to do his dealings. I swear to god if he's harmed her in any way he is as good as dead. The road to prosperity wasn't easy for Maya. She failed many times on her way to recovery. She had lost a great deal of weight and nothing mattered to her except getting high. I battled for her. I fought her demons along with her. If her demons have returned will she have anything left in her to fight them off? For five years I peddled drugs for that bastard. When I took the fall not once did he come visit me in prison? Instead, he sent his piss boy Xavier to keep tabs on me. The lone thing that concerned him was if I would open my mouth to the feds. He and Xavier both knew I wasn't a snitch. I would die in prison before opening my mouth. Half the prison population at one time or another worked for Darius's father.

Mr. Reed carries himself like a legit business man, but underneath the glitter and shiny suits is a stone cold killer willing to do anything to make a profit. The mentioning of his name makes most people in the city cringe. Darius is his only son. He runs his day to day operations. His chief dealings are drugs and prostitution, but his dirty hands are into other illegal activities as well. Nearly every building in the city belongs to Mr. Reed in one way or another, and if he doesn't own it the proprietors are paying him a hefty price to operate in his area. Rumor has it many of the police force is on his payroll. Mr. Reed taught Darius how to become a shrewd and tenacious street thug. When I worked for Darius I learned from firsthand experience how vicious he can be. His clan of misfits with Xavier as his right hand man carries out his commands without discretion. When Maya came into our circle buying drugs for leisure with her college girlfriends, Xavier and I both had a thing for Maya in the beginning. He hated the fact she chose me instead of him. I sold Marijuana to Maya. I didn't want her to become an addict by giving her anything harsher. We smoked weed together and consumed each other on many occasions to the dismay of Xavier. It hurt him to see us together, so he plotted against me to pull Maya away. Xavier forced heroin into her body. Maya became a drug addict because of him. I nearly killed him from his vicious act of treachery. If it wasn't for Maya pleading with me not to do it, his life would have been over. With his henchmen running loose I have to find her before they do. I'll try her number again. Lord, please let her answer.

"Hello." *It feels so good to hear her voice.*

"Maya, I need to see you. It's urgent."

"You're too late Julius. I told you what would happen if I didn't get my money. You know I always follow through."

"Ok, ok, Darius. I will get you the money. Just don't hurt her. Please don't hurt her."

"It's too late for that. You should've thought of that before you betrayed me."

CHAPTER 25

JODIE

"Julia is here in Baltimore."

"Are you sure Jodie? Have you physically seen her?"

"I haven't physically seen her, but I know her work. She's starting this crap all over again."

"What kind of details do you have to suggest this?"

"Do you remember my girlfriend Maya from college?"

"Yes, I remember her."

"Well, Julia has been sleeping with her fiancé to implicate me."

"Why would she do such a thing?"

"To make my life miserable I suppose. Maya must really despise me. That's why she's been so cold to me. She thinks I'm sleeping with her man and she hates me for dating her brother."

"Jeffrey is Maya's brother?"

"Yes."

"What if Julia has her claws in Jeffrey also?"

"Mother, I hope not. I love Jeffrey. It's bad enough Maya and her mother are conspiring against me to keep Jeffrey away from me. They have brought in another woman who's pretending to be his girlfriend. This sham has been staged by both of them. Maya feels I'm no good for her brother and so does her mother."

"Isn't her mother a pastor of the church?"

"Yes. But what does that mean? She sins like everyone else, cloak or no cloak."

"What will you do?"

"I have to find Julia before she makes her next move. She's walking around pretending to be me, and only God knows what she has done so far."

"I exiled her years ago for a reason. Why is she still causing trouble for us?"

139

"Mother, I don't have an answer. I think you should notify my brothers. If she's on my heels I can only assume she will be following them next."

"I've been trying to figure her out for years Jodie. I've given her everything. Why is she so vindictive?"

"Like I stated before, I don't have any answers. But, I need to find some in a hurry."

"You just be careful. She's not playing with a full deck of cards. I will tell your father she's on the prowl again. We will be on the lookout. Neither of us has the slightest clue into what she is planning. I have a hunch it pertains to money in some form or fashion."

"Money?"

"Yes, your sister will do anything to get it. Remember when she was caught stealing a man's wallet at the age of 13?"

"I remember somewhat. I know she was punished for it. She couldn't go outside for at least a month."

"Do you know after her punishment was over she went right back to stealing again? This time, she stole from an elderly woman, confiscating fifty dollars out of her purse. If Julia doesn't get what she wants she manages to find a way to get it. When I handed out allowance money to each of you, Julia would save hers and never spend a dime of it. She held onto money like no one I ever seen. Do you know by the end of the year your sister had accumulated more than five hundred dollars in allowance money?"

"I never knew that."

"When it comes to money Julia will do anything to get her hands on it."

"Do you really believe money is behind this?"

"I certainly do. How well is Julius financially?"

"Julius is a city bus driver. He makes decent pay, but he's no Sean Combs."

"He has to be connected to money in some form or fashion. If he isn't, Julia wouldn't waste her time with him. What about Jeffrey? How lucrative is his portfolio?"

"Jeffrey is the CEO of a software company. He has stocks and other investments along with his six figure salary."

"Be very careful Jodie, your sister is looking to cash out. She's using you to get her big payday."

"This is definitely not a coincidence. Do you think she studied them in advance?"

"I really do think so. She's found a payday at your expense. Why else would she be here? If you want to find her, follow the money trail."

"I wonder how many others she is planning to steal from."

"I'm sure it's a lot. Focus your attention on Julius for a while. Find out if he has money. She won't stop until she cleans him out."

"I will try my best."

"I know you will. I don't doubt you."

"Mother, you and dad be careful. I will call you when I find out further information."

"Take care of yourself Jodie."

"Mother, you do the same."

Julia, I know you're out there somewhere. I will find you and put a stop to your plans. Were twins, or did you forget? I know exactly how you think, and my intuition is telling me you'll come for Jeffrey in due time. If you think for a minute I will sit idle and let you take him from me then you have really lost your mind. He belongs to me, not you, nor Vanessa. He's mine. So get it through your cracked skull. Jeffrey and I love each other and have plans to start a family. I suggest you go back to wherever it is you came from. You're not wanted here. One Jodie in Baltimore is more than enough. There isn't any room for two. You can try me if you want to, nevertheless I will be waiting to send you back to your previous destination. I know you can hear me, were only two minutes apart from birth. If you decide to come, I will be right here waiting for you.

"Hello?"

"Julius, it's me."

"I thought I told you to leave me alone Jodie."

"I am leaving you alone."

"How are you leaving me alone when you're constantly calling me?"

"I want to know your progress on getting me in to see Jeffrey."

"It's going to take a minute. I can't find Maya."

"Maya's missing?"

"Not exactly, I have to do some ass kissing to see her."

"Julius, I'm sorry for the inconvenience I caused. I truly want us to stay friends. I know you hate me and all, but can you forgive me?"

"I forgive you Jodie. Just don't come near me."

"What do you want me to do, beg? I promise I will be good from now on. All I'm asking is for an opportunity to get together once and a while."

"I really believe you're delusional. I will not jeopardize my chances of getting Maya back by being with you. Just stay away Jodie. That's the best thing you can do for me."

"Didn't we have something special at one time? You can't just ignore it?"

"I can ignore it, and I will ignore it. It was only lust."

"When you decide to come around Julius I will be here to listen. I don't want to lose our friendship."

"Friendship? You call what we have a friendship? Jodie, the only thing we have in common is in the bedroom. We consume each other most of the time. We never really talk about anything important. It's like were strangers."

CHAPTER 26

MAYA

"Maya I must say you have really taken care of yourself. You look better than ever. It angers me to know you chose Julius over me. I told you I would've taken care of you." *What makes him think I ever wanted him in the first place? He's nothing but a low life piece of scum.*

"I find that quite amusing. How were you supposed to take care of me when you didn't have a job or even a high school diploma?"

"I think school is highly overrated. For example, there are thousands of college graduates working for little to nothing. Many of them have moved back home with mommy and daddy because they don't make enough to make ends meet. This country has sold its citizens a pipe dream. The reality is everyone is in debt paying student loans they can't afford to pay. I don't have to ever worry about that. Words on a page don't make a person. It's what's inside of them that make the person."

"You have nothing inside of you that I want."

"You and I both know that's a lie."

"Well, I'm sorry to burst your bubble, but I only have eyes for Julius." *And as of late, my eyes are beginning to see the truth in Julius.* Xavier, you never appealed to me at all. You're not my type. Besides, I like tall men."

"I might be shorter than Julius, but I'm stretched out in other areas."

"Maya, Xavier has always been attracted to you. As a matter of fact he talks of nothing else. Every woman he's been with doesn't compare to you. Don't you think we should do something about that?"

"I think the both of you should release me. Why do you have me tied up in the first place? I've done nothing to either of you."

"Julius owes me money. He stole from me and in return I took something valuable of his. And from the looks of things you're definitely worth the money. I can make a lot of money off of you." *Darius is starting to frighten me. The sight of his delirious bloodshot eyes makes my stomach churn. What has Julius done to me?"*

"Darius, whatever he owes you, I'm sure he will pay it back."

"He did promise to pay it back, but the promise came much too late for my liking."

"Let me call him and he will bring the money to you."

"His grace period is over. I have to teach him a lesson. X, will you do the honors?"

"Certainly boss."

"What's that in your hand Xavier?"

"Don't play dumb Maya. You're college educated, remember? You know exactly what's in my hand. It's your medicine. I hear you haven't tasted it in a while, but as the saying goes, once an addict always an addict. Isn't that right Maya?"

"I wouldn't know. I'm free from drugs," he devilishly grins.

"Well, I think it's time for you to get reacquainted again." *I've fought so hard to become drug free. I can't go back to being an addict again. They have to stop. God, please make them stop.*

"Someone help me, please help me!"

"You can scream all you want Maya if that's what you like, but no one will help you. I own this building and all of the people in it."

"Get that needle away from me Xavier! Julius will kill you for this Darius. You know how much you're afraid of him. Are you willing to die Darius? Because that's what will happen, you will die by his hands," he glares at me.

"X, shut this bitch up. I'm tired of her mouth already."

"Here's something to quiet you Maya."

"No, no, no, get it away from me. Get it away from me! Ok, ok, ok, I'll do whatever you want. I'll be your woman Xavier. I'll let you take care of me. You can have me. You can have all of me. Darius I beg you, don't let him do this to me."

"Hold up X. Did she just say she would be your woman? Did I hear her correctly? After all the years you wanted her?"

"Hell yeah, I believe she did."

"Maya, are you lying to us?"

"No Darius, I'm serious, Xavier can have me. I will do whatever he wants me to do."

"Then shut the hell up and let him give you your medicine." *As I cry out for help I can feel the syringe penetrating my vein working deeper into my arm. Suddenly a rush accompanied by a warm sensation over my skin is surging through my entire body. The pleasurable sensation begins to weaken my extremities. My heartrate and breathing is severely slowed. The Heroin begins to counteract my senses as I gradually become unaware of my surroundings. The monster I fought so hard to get away from is tormenting me again. God if you can hear me don't allow me to become an addict again. I've lost too much in the past because of it. Please take vengeance on them for doing this to me. I beg you please.*

"Just look at her X. She looks so peaceful."

"What do we do with her now?"

"I thought I already told you what were gonna do with her."

"I didn't think you really meant it," puzzlement spreads across Darius's face.

"X, what the hell is my name?"

"Darius."

"If you know my name, then you know when I say something I mean what I say."

"I just thought."

"Don't think," Darius interrupts him. "Are you getting soft on me X?"

"No. I'm down for whatever."

"I know what's wrong. You still want her don't you? It's all over your face."

"Na, na, I'm good. She belongs to Julius anyway. She was never mine to begin with."

"Don't let a piece of ass make you lose focus. We have to teach that nigga a lesson."

"Ok, I will take her there now. Are they expecting her?"

"Yes, everything's set up. All you have to do is to drop her ass off and make sure you're not followed."

"I got it."

"And one more thing, I need you to pay his mother a visit as well."

"His mother?"

"Nigga, don't look like you just seen a ghost. I said his mother."

"What... what... do you want me to do to his mother?"

"Make her suffer some. Don't kill her though; just beat up on her a little. Some bruises and shit like that. Do you think you can handle that? Or do you want me to send Mo and Freddy?"

"No, I will take care of it."

"I hope so. Don't make it a problem. Business is business. It's how my father and I stay in power. We put fear in those who go against us. I hope you're not one of those."

"Why would I be? I've been putting in work for you for years Darius. Why do you doubt me?"

"It's because of her that I have doubts in your duties."

"There's no need to fret. I will deliver her to the brothel."

"Dalilah will be waiting for you. Bring her through the back entrance."

"Xavier.... stop....please....help....me."

"X, get her out of here. Call me when it's done. And remember, watch your back. Julius is probably lurking around."

"That nigga doesn't frighten me."

"The Julius that I know will come with everything."

CHAPTER 27

JEFFREY

As Jodie chauffeurs me through the city I'm trying every effort to remember her. To say she is beautiful is simply not enough to fully describe her. I'm overtaken by her appearance. When she smiles my world seems to stop moving. How did I ever manage to pull someone with her qualities? I want to remember her and recapture what we once had together. She's taking me to the software company I currently work for and then my home. If these two places can't help me remember who I am then I'm a lost case. She said it should. And that I need to focus on my surroundings which may open up my past.

"Were here handsome, I hope this helps," she pulls into the parking lot. "Does anything look familiar to you?" *I hate to disappoint, but I don't recognize anything. The building is a massive skyscraper. Jodie informed me the company produces similar products as Microsoft.*

"I'm sorry Jodie but my mind is blank. But I have an idea, what if I ask you more about my position. It may open up the floodgates to help me remember."

"That sounds perfect. Let's give it a shot. Ask me something," she smiles moving the long strands of hair out of her face.

"What is my position?"

"Jeffrey, you're the CEO of the company."

"What types of duties are required of the CEO?"

"Well for starters, you oversee about a thousand employees. As a matter of fact, you strive on providing a productive atmosphere for your staff. On several occasions you disguised yourself as a regular employee similar to the show undercover boss to get a better feel of what kind of individuals are working for the company, and what can be done to boost work morale."

"What about the products?"

"The software being produced is cut of the edge technology; from anti-virus programs, games developed for computers, as well as cell phone chips. Your company is a leading conglomerate in the software industry."

"Wow, I must say you know quite a bit about the business."

"Well, my fiancé tells me everything. He doesn't keep anything from me. He trusts me and I completely trust him."

"This fiancé of yours, how do you feel about him?"

"He's my world and then some. I must get him back. It's been difficult for me to function without him."

"How did you meet him?" She unbuckles her seat belt leaning in closer to me.

"I met him through my girlfriend, which is his sister. I had a deranged person stalking me. My girlfriend Maya insisted on using her brothers to get rid of him. When they completed the job one of her brothers approached me about going out together. I agreed, and we have been with each other ever since."

"Is he everything you ever wanted?" Her lips are inches from mine.

"Yes, and then some," I swallow hard.

"Is he a good kisser?"

"He's the best."

"Can he show you now?"

"He certainly can," *I close my eyes allowing Jodie to explore my mouth with her tongue. Our lips are firmly pressed together generating a warm friction. She's a passionate kisser knowing how to tantalize me.*

"Vanessa, please don't stop kissing me. I love the way you kiss me," *Jodie abruptly pulls away from me as if I'm contagious.*

"I can't believe you called me by her name."

"Who are you talking about?"

"Vanessa."

"I did not call you Vanessa. I called you by your name, Jodie. I know I did."

"You did not Jeffrey. Don't you remember?"

"How the hell can I know what I just said when I'm suffering from a concussion? That's the problem Jodie, I can't remember. I can't recall anything. I don't know what I'm saying half the time. Please don't confuse me anymore than I already am," *she looks hurt. I didn't mean to offend her.*"

"Jeffrey, let's just go to your home. Forget about it ok? She snaps on her seatbelt putting the car in drive and proceeds to fly through the parking lot.

"I'm sorry if I unintentionally spoke her name. It was a mistake." *After my major debacle the ride to my home is nothing but silence. Jodie refuses to interact with me. Her attention remains on the road. When we arrive to my place Jodie doesn't speak at all and points at the house. We simultaneously get out of the car and she tosses me the keys. My home has a nice touch to it. It boarders the harbor by at least a mile in distance and is set in a small secluded village on the mainland. I can smell the seawater and hear the sounds of the boats traversing through the water. This is great place to live. How can I not remember it? I follow Jodie to the front door. I try turning the key, but the key doesn't work. I give it three more attempts only to get the same results.*

"Jodie, are you sure this is the right key?" She frowns.

"I'm positive this is the right key. I've used it several times myself. Give me the key, let me try. Sometimes you have to jiggle it a little," she puts the key inside the lock and jiggles it a few times, but nothing happens.

"I guess it's the wrong key then."

"It's not the wrong key. Your mother and sister probably changed the locks."

"Do you honestly believe they would go that far?" She shakes her head in disbelief.

"They brought in Vanessa, so why wouldn't they change the locks?" Jodie slams her fists against the front door and begins to cry.

"They're trying to get rid of me Jeffrey, and I believe it's working. We will never be together again." *Watching her carry out in this manner touches my heart. I hate to see anyone cry, especially her. I wish I could remember something. There's also the possibility she can be lying to me. Why would I give her a key to my place that doesn't work? Is she pulling a fast one on me? Is this all an act? Her tears have smeared her mascara. I grab onto her slumping body.*

"It's alright Jodie. We will find another way for me to remember."

"I want to believe that, but nothing is working," I wipe away her tears.

"It will work out. If this is meant to be, nothing will prevent it from happening."

"I hope you're right."

"I know I'm right."

"Would you like me to bring you back?"

"No, let's go to your place instead. There's other ways for me to remember."

"I like the suggestion."

I'm confused at this point as to what is happening to me. Is Jodie being genuine? Or is there something sinister brewing behind her beauty? Did my mother and sister actually bring in Vanessa to get rid of Jodie? And if so, what is the underlying reason? Vanessa is a great person but so is Jodie. They're both beautiful, and I'm attracted to each of them. As the saying goes, beauty is only skin deep. If that's certain, when the looks slowly deteriorate and old age begins to set in along with the wrinkles, will their hearts be unaffected by the change? I need a woman who is willing to be there for me in good times and bad times. I need a woman to support me if I am unable to. Her heart has to be sincere. How do I know who is being honest and who is being dishonest? The truth will present itself eventually.

Maybe by then, my memory will be fully restored. In the meantime I have to make a decision concerning which woman I want to be with. I could stay with Jodie until my memory returns. She will definitely be delighted with my choice. On the other hand, Vanessa is just as important to me. If I choose to stay with her she will also be thrilled. If I can just remember something, or anything, it will help me into making a valid decision. It's not right for me to have sex with her not knowing fully who she is. As bad as I want to, I must use discretion. Vanessa has been good to me as of so far. She's been in my corner fighting my battles with me. I will not disrespect her. I need to find out the truth. I tell Jodie to bring me back instead of going to her place. She doesn't look happy, although she will understand in the long run.

CHAPTER 28

JULIUS

I've never realized how much Maya has meant to me until the time of her absence. I received a call just a few days ago from Darius. He has taken Maya and won't give up the location where he is keeping her. I think he has her drugged. She sounded disoriented when I spoke with her briefly. I pleaded with Darius to let her go, but he refused to do so. I even offered to pay what I owe him. He said the price increased due to the fact I held out on him. Now he wants fifty large. The fifty large is not the problem for me. Darius is the real problem. If I give into paying him the money he will keep increasing it just to prove to me he has control over me. He'll never settle for a set price, it's just the manner in which he operates. He's nothing like his father. Don't get me wrong, his father is a piece of scum as Darius, nonetheless at least he has morals. Darius on the other hand doesn't play by the rules. I've worked with all his so called tough guys that protect him. He never travels alone. There's only one way to handle this. I don't have any other option if I ever want to see Maya again.

Darius will never accept any amount of money I offer to him. He will continue to play games and frustrate me more and more. The only other alternative I have is to go see his father. Maybe I can settle the debt with him instead. Setting up a meeting with Darius's father is like walking into a lion's den. He's heavily guarded twenty four hours a day and doesn't allow too many people to get near him. At one time he considered me family. When I stopped peddling drugs for Darius I think it angered him. Before my decision to quit his father stayed in touch with me. He told me if I ever needed anything don't hesitate to ask him. He treated me like a son. That was then, when things were different. I hope his open generosity is still valid.

There was once a time in my life when I would've killed a man for looking at me the wrong way. My temper was uncontrollable. When I sold drugs for Darius I also did other odd inhumane jobs on the side if it was required of me. I've killed a man before. Not just one, but at least a few. It's something I'm not proud of. I had no choice. My hand was forced. When you work for Darius's family your loyalty is depended on. To test your loyalty you're required to kill someone for them. It can be anyone. When they assign you to do the job you must accept if you want employment. I killed a father of three which haunts me to this very day. I had to shoot him in front of his family, in the head.

His terrifying face still haunts my sleep. I have many sleepless nights because of it. After taking the first life, pulling the trigger on others became easier. The gun gave me a sense of invincibility. When I decided to get away from that life I sought out therapy. Joining Maya's father's church took away the nightmares and the guilt I felt. Now she's gone and I'm responsible for everything. I have to make all the wrongs I've done right. My Maxima looks like it came out of a car showroom. The body shop did a wonderful job restoring it after Benny went ballistic. The car seems to handle better than before. While driving through the city I feel nervous as ever, something that's not part of my character. I learned how to be ruthless when I worked the streets. I never fear anyone, or anything.

In the streets, fear is a handicap that can get you buried six feet deep in a heartbeat. I guess it's a normal emotion all of us carry inside of us when the odds of life are not in our favor. We become frightened by outside circumstances. I definitely don't like feeling this way, then again I know the road ahead of me will be a difficult one to travel. Darius's father lives in a lavish penthouse just outside of Maryland. He has accumulated most of his wealth illegally. The youngsters in the inner city call him the candy man. He hands out candy to children every first of the month. He thinks he's Robin Hood or something. Instead of robbing from the rich and giving to the poor, he steals from the poor by destroying their lives and making them dependent on drugs. Their dependency robs the neighborhood as they confiscate anything to barter for drugs while leaving the community in shambles. When I arrive I have to pass through a series of checkpoints before reaching Darius's father.

In the first checkpoint two guards pat me down for weapons. In the second, two more guards use scanners to check for electronic devices. In the third checkpoint, I have to remove my clothing as they check for wires and hidden cameras on my body. To say his father is paranoid is an understatement. He believes he is being targeted at all times. When you've killed and robbed as many people as he has, I assume you can never trust anyone. Not even your family. After the rigorous surveillance I'm finally allowed to enter Mr. Reed's pool area. There are a couple women swimming naked inside the built in pool. I can't help but stare because of their attractiveness. The one closest to me is African American and her bodily dimensions are astounding as she swims past me. Her companion inside the pool with her is white. She is just as gorgeous as the black girl, but I can't see her face. Whatever Mr. Reed has is always the best. I'm so transfixed on ebony and ivory I don't hear Mr. Reed walk up on me.

"Julius, are you enjoying yourself?" His voice startles me. I feel slightly embarrassed turning around to face him. He looks clean cut as usual, wearing white swimming trunks with white sandals and a towel wrapped around his almond colored shoulders.

"I'm sorry Mr. Reed. I was."

"You don't have to explain. I know they're both beautiful. Everyone else seems to think so, including me. I let them walk around my penthouse as they please. I feel more comfortable when their naked. There's nothing they can hide from me."

"Isn't it hard to concentrate with their bodies exposed like that?" *I sneak in another peek to get a glimpse at ivory's face. She's close to turning around in the pool.*

"You get used to it after a while. Once you've seen one you've seen them all. So what brings you to my abode?"

"I have a major problem Mr. Reed. I'm sure you already know about it."

"There's not too much I don't know, especially when it comes to my business. A debt is a debt Julius."

"It's the reason why I'm here. I was wondering if I can pay you the debt instead. Your son refuses to take my offer."

"He raised the price because you reneged on the money. You deliberately wouldn't pay him. So the price has doubled."

"How do I know he won't continue to raise it?"

"You have no idea of knowing that."

"Can you stop him from increasing it? I have to get Maya back," he looks at me startled.

"Why do you want her back?"

"I love her Mr. Reed."

"In my position Julius I hear a lot of things. It's one of the means to help me stay in business. I hear you're seeing someone else. How can you say you love Maya when you're dealing with another woman? I don't consider that love. How can you?"

"I made a mistake in judgement. We all make mistakes," he smiles at the women inside the pool. *And Ivory's face causes me to lose my balance.*

"Julius, remember when you played ball?"

"Yes." *How can she be here with this monster? What kind of woman is she? Is she doing this to torture me more than I already am? What is her angle? I know she has to have one. She is definitely playing with fire and will soon be consumed by it.*

"You were extremely talented. I'm certain you would've made the NBA if things worked out differently. A mistake, a bad decision, an awful choice in judgement, whatever you want to call it, it's the reason why you're here, isn't it?"

"Yes it is."

"If only you took care of matters more important than women you wouldn't be in this predicament. Let me not dwell on it. It's behind you now. You must realize when we make a mistake sometimes we have to pay a hefty price for it. Whatever your debt is I feel it's necessary you pay it. It's how the Reed family takes care of business. Do I make myself clear?" *I dare not go against Mr. Reed in front of him. As angry as I am inside I know my place. If he doesn't want to help me I will have to take matters in my own hands. If Maya is hurt in any way I will make all of them pay for it, including Mr. Reed. He doesn't scare me, although I'm no fool either.*

"Crystal."

"By the way, I would like you to meet Abigail. We've been seeing each other for quite some time. Baby, get out of the pool. I would like you to meet someone." *Her name isn't Abigail, its Jodie. Jodie climbs out of the pool with nothing covering her body but warm dripping water. She strolls up to Mr. Reed kissing him without ever taking her eyes off of him. I can feel her lust through my bones.*

"Abigail, this is Julius. He used to work for us," he covers her up with the towel.

"Hi," she extends her wet hands. I want to break all her fingers, but I shake her hand politely in return. "Are you planning to work for us again?" She smirks.

"No, I have job. Mr. Reed and I were just discussing small talk," she rings out her mane as the water patters against the concrete. *She's deliberately taunting me. She's on her own finding Jeffrey. She will never get any of my help ever again.*

"Well, nice to meet you. Honey, I'll be inside. Aren't you coming in to join me?"

"I'll be there shortly. Don't get started without me."

"Well hurry up, I don't know if I can hold out any longer," she walks off. *I can't believe the nerve of her. How can she do this?*

"That woman has reinvigorated my spirit. She's fifteen years younger than me, but I can handle her. She never gets tired of sex. And lately, it's all I've been thinking about. I feel as if I'm ten years younger. She's food for the soul." *As he speaks to me his words are falling on deaf ears. I reject anything he has to say. For Mr. Reed not to help my situation is disheartening to me. He is blatantly allowing his son to dictate to me. He could have settled it right here and now. I would've paid him the money with interest. If he thinks for one second I will tolerate Darius's games he has me confused with someone else. If he doesn't want to put a stop to this, then I will.*

"Julius, I expect you to take care of your obligation. I hope there are no hard feelings between us," *he's trying to read me. I keep a poker face in front of him.*

"There are no hard feelings between us Mr. Reed."

Thanks for purchasing forbidden part 1. I hope you enjoyed the story. Please don't hesitate to write a review. Once again, thank you for your patronage. The following is an excerpt from Forbidden Part 2, Mask of Deception.

FORBIDDEN

PART 2

MASK OF DECEPTION
BY EDMOND WHITE

DEDICATION

Again, I would like to thank God for his favor and mercy. He has helped me in countless times. Without him none of this would be possible. I write because it is something I love to do. I enjoy creating stories for readers throughout the world. I began this journey of writing a number of years ago, and I have to say your responses have been awesome. I will continue to push out stories and improve along the way. I would like to thank you for purchasing my work. IT IS MUCH APPRECIATED. I dedicate this story to my longtime friend Mr. Tracy Lamb. I MISS YOU BRUH! REST IN PEACE.

PROLOGUE

A promiscuous woman is as dangerous as falling into a narrow well.
She hides and waits like a robber, eager to make more men unfaithful.
Proverbs 23:27-28

CHAPTER 1

JODIE

What is Julia's next move? If only I knew her whereabouts? To find Julia I must think like her. My mother insists she's after money. She's been sleeping with Julius for God knows how long. I pray to God she hasn't touched Jeffrey. If she has I will be terribly disappointed. Maya never talked of Julius having any substantial amount of money. He has a decent job to make a living but that's about it. Does he have some kind of inheritance? Did he hit the lottery? What kind of money can he actually have? I know for a fact Maya has told me everything about him. Then again, maybe she hasn't. Does his money have something to do with her? I bet she deliberately kept it from me so she wouldn't implicate herself? Is Julius involved in something illegal? I know he played collegiate basketball and could have gone professional, but the injury thing prevented him from going any further.

What were his career options after basketball failed to pan out for him? Most athletes today do not have a backup plan if the sports thing doesn't work out. It must have hurt him entirely knowing he wouldn't be able to play professional ball and have a chance to accumulate millions. Did he settle for illegal money instead? How much money does he actually have, and how did he attain it? Today, you can google everything. I pick up my I-phone and google Julius Miles of Georgetown University. It reads Julius Channing Miles suffers a torn ACL which ends his collegiate basketball career and chances of turning pro. His attempts at rehabbing his knew went unsuccessful and he eventually dropped out of college. Two years later Mr. Miles was arrested for selling heroin on the streets and served time in jail. A drug dealer, that's it? Julius has drug money and probably lots of it to attract my thieving sister.

Where does he have it stashed? Maya never spoke of it. She probably doesn't know where it is or any clue it exists. How does my sister know? How does she know about Julius's supply of cash? I have to warn Julius.

I have to let him know I have a twin sister. He will probably think I'm insane. I have to give it a shot. I tap in his cell number. He answers on the second ring.

"Hello?"

"Julius, we need to talk."

"Jodie, you're becoming a living nightmare for me. I just saw your whorish ass with Mr. Reed. Why the hell are you calling me? Mr. Reed is the wrong person to play games with. I've said what I had to say already. You're really crazy. Stay away from me. You hear me! Stay the hell away!"

"You saw my sister."

"Your sister?"

"Yes. I have a twin and I can't believe she's involved with Mr. Reed."

"A twin? You mean to tell me there are two of you bitches?"

"I'm the good one Julius."

"And how am I supposed to believe that?"

"You just have to trust me on this."

"I don't trust anything that comes out of your mouth woman. I'm done with your lies. Do you think I'm a fool Jodie, or is it Abigail?"

"Abigail? Why do you think my name is Abigail?"

"You tell me. That's what Mr. Reed called you, isn't it?"

"He called my sister that."

"Cut the sister crap out! It's you. It's always been you."

"It's never been me Julius. To prove it to you let's meet somewhere so I can explain."

"That, I'm sorry will never happen. I can't trust you. No more, not ever."

"Were identical twins and my sister has an identifying mark that separates us from birth. It's a small discoloration inside of her eye. It's only apparent when she looks to her right side. It's the left eye. Make sure you look at that one. It's the only way to tell us apart."

"You expect me to believe this shit, a mark inside your sister's eye? Woman you will come up with anything won't you?"

"You have to believe me on this. My sister is dangerous. She's after the money."

"What money?"

"The drug money. The money you made when you sold heroin on the streets."

"The money is long gone and there's nothing left."

"Julius, I believe there's a lot of it left. I believe it's hidden somewhere."

"Are you done woman? I have to go."

"I'm not done Julius. I want you to listen to me. You need to pay close attention. My sister won't stop bothering you until she gets the cash. I can help you though. Better yet, we can help each other and put an end to her plans."

"Look, you're wasting your time."

"We need to act on this in a hurry before it's too late. Knowing Julia, it's probably already too late."

"Ok, even if I did have a stash of drug money as you're suggesting, I would never let you near it or anyone else for that matter."

"Please just listen to me. I know my sister. She will clean you out."

"Look Jodie, Julia, or is it Abigail? Like I said, leave me the hell alone. I'm finished with you. Don't you get it? It's over. Walk away before I permanently force you to walk away."

"If that's how you want to play this good luck. Mark my words Julius. When my sister is finished with you, trust, you will beg for my help."

"Is that it? Are you done?"

"Yes, I think I am. Julia sure the hell isn't."

Julius is a stubborn bastard. Why wouldn't he listen to me? I did my best to make him understand. When will men ever listen to us? The only time men pay attention is when our legs are spread wide apart for them.

Forget Julius, he will come looking for me in a matter of time. For now I have to find Julia. Mr. Reed owns half of Baltimore. He is well known and well disliked by most of the residents. It's rumored Mr. Reed has a particular obsession for white women. How convenient for me considering Julia has her hooks in him already. I can show up at his place pretending to be Julia. He will never know the difference. I just have to make certain Julia is not around. She's been pretending to be me for God knows how long. It's time I return the favor. Mr. Reed will never suspect anything. If I can get close to him I will find out where Julia is staying. Mr. Reed owns a popular night club on Crenshaw Avenue called Club Ecstasy.

It's one of his prized establishments where he is highly visible. I just need to be me and I can get inside the club without much of an effort. Once they see my face Mr. Reed's bouncers will assume I'm Julia, or her street name Abigail. Friday night will be perfect. It's ladies night. The first fifty women get in free before ten o'clock. I will wear something enticing. When I strut inside Club Ecstasy everyone will notice me. I will have to turn up my sophisticated act in the presence of Mr. Reed. I hope he doesn't want anything in return. I don't believe in sleeping around. I just need information and then I'm out of there. It won't be easy pretending to be someone as heartless as my sister. She has no morals, manners, and not an ounce of empathy for anyone, including her family. Julia's world of deception must come to an end. It's time for her to pay for what she has done to others. My sister has committed her last crime. I will put an end to everything. Julia, it's time I give you some of your own medicine. I wonder how it will taste. I hope it burns a hole in your twisted black heart. It would have been nice to have a normal twin sister identical to me in every form and fashion. You could have been my youthful playmate, trusted friend, motherly voice, and a sister there for me in any circumstance. I had your back but you never had mine. As the saying goes; revenge is a bitch.

CHAPTER 2

Dalilah sits nervously at the front desk contemplating her next move. She runs her business in a professional manner. Her girls work around the clock to fulfill her reliable customers. When the call came in from Darius her instincts cautioned it would be troubling, although she couldn't refuse his demand. Dalilah works for his father. Mr. Reed protects her business from the feds. Customers with substantial bank accounts and deep pockets keep her brothel running problem free. Dalilah's relationship with her paying clientele remains professional at all times. She has rigid standards for each of her girls to follow. Dalilah never involves herself sexually with the clients. She never mixes business with pleasure. Men entering the brothel choosing their woman of choice oftentimes are interested in Dalilah more so than her girls.

At fifty years of age Dalilah has a curvy figure and enticing misty brown eyes. She is frequently mistaken as one of the call girls instead of Madame of the house. Not long ago a call girl herself, Dalilah learned how to maintain her exquisite form and undeniable pure attractiveness. People close to her say she looks a lot like the actress/singer Vanessa Williams. As Dalilah sits at the front desk she worries about the woman Darius brought in a few days ago. How is she expected to run her business with this major distraction? She prides herself into pleasing men and not kidnapping and rape. Darius's stringent instructions is to have this woman drugged twenty-four hours a day allowing his men to do whatever they please with her.

As a woman herself Dalilah absolutely disagrees with this. How can she allow this female to be raped inside of her brothel each day? She discerns it's wrong but dare not go against Mr. Reed. He has a strong hold on every business in the city. Whatever he wants he usually gets or the consequences will be severe for many of the proprietors in the city. Darius informed her he would send a different goon each day. The ill-fated young woman is beautiful to Dalilah. What a shame she reasons. Every few hours before the drug wears off Dalilah dreads sticking the syringe filled with heroin deep into the woman's veins. Most of the men Darius sends over are nothing but low life scum to Dalilah, preferably young ignorant drug dealers still wet behind the ears. It hurts her to know their raping this woman inside of her establishment. What has she done to warrant this atrocity? She must have family. Someone has to be looking for her. They have probably filed a missing person's report. Dalilah doesn't need the police snooping around her place. Whatever this woman has done Darius needs to get her out of here immediately. She refuses to go to jail over this. It has taken her years to construct her profitable business.

She will not let it crash and burn to the ground because of Darius's carelessness. The young thug inside the room where the woman is being held has been inside over an hour. Normally these inexperienced fools come out in at least fifteen minutes. Dalilah dreads going inside the room, but she has an unnerving feeling something terrible has occurred. If she has died what will she do with a dead woman inside her brothel? She never wanted this trouble brought to her. It's just too risky. Dalilah reaches for her 9mm Glock and silencer positioned securely underneath the front desk. She attaches the silencer taking off the safety heading down to the basement. Dalilah travels prudently along the corridor stopping in front of the desolate looking room. She puts her ear against the faded red door. Dalilah hears the sounds of intense pleasure coming from the young thug. As she listens more intensely she overhears subdued screams coming from the woman. Dalilah turns the door knob opening the door delicately. She stands in the doorway in terror from what is happening.

The drama continues as Jodie tries to find her way back into Jeffrey's life. Will Jeffrey ever remember her, or will his mother sabotage Jodie's plan to reunite with him? Will Maya be rescued from her kidnapping? Can Julius come to her aide in time? Does Julius go against Mr. Reed in his efforts to find Maya? Can he afford to ignore Mr. Reed's command? How does Jeffrey decide which woman is telling the truth? Who can he trust? Forbidden Part 2, THE MASK OF DECEPTION, will reveal all of the answers. AVAILABLE NOW ON AMAZON.COM